"GEORGES DE PEYT
onym of Mathilde-Ma
Peyrebrune (1841-191?
included *Marco* (1882),
(1885), and *Les Ensevelis* (...narily
serialized in the *Revue des   Mondes*, where
she had made her debut. Though friends with
many avant-garde writers, such as Rachilde, she
generally chose the path of "respectable fiction,"
two of her novels being crowned by the Académie
française. She was part of the first jury for the Prix
Fémina in 1905. Though one of the most popular
writers of her day, she died in poverty.

BRIAN STABLEFORD'S scholarly work in-
cludes *New Atlantis: A Narrative History of Scientific Romance* (Wildside Press, 2016), *The Plurality
of Imaginary Worlds: The Evolution of French roman
scientifique* (Black Coat Press, 2017) and *Tales of
Enchantment and Disenchantment: A History of
Faerie* (Black Coat Press, 2019). In support of the
latter projects he has translated more than a hundred volumes of *roman scientifique* and more than
twenty volumes of *contes de fées* into English.

SNUGGLY BOOKS

GEORGES DE PEYREBRUNE

A DECADENT WOMAN

TRANSLATED AND WITH AN INTRODUCTION BY
BRIAN STABLEFORD

THIS IS A SNUGGLY BOOK

ISBN: 978-1-64525-061-6

CONTENTS

INTRODUCTION

"UNE DÉCADENTE" by "Georges de Peyrebrune" (1841-1917), here translated as "A Decadent Woman" was initially published in two parts in the *Revue Bleue* in the issues for 20 mars and 27 mars 1886. "Les Fées" (tr. as "The Fays") appeared in book form as a supplement to the short novel *Giselle* (1891) and in the literary supplement to *L'Écho de Paris* in the same year; it had presumably appeared previously in another periodical which I have not been able to identify. "L'Oiseau rouge" (tr, as "The Red Bird") and "Salomé" (tr. as Salome") both appeared for the first time in *L'Écho de Paris* in 1889, in the issues for 19 septembre and 27 décembre respectively.

Madame de Peyrebrune—whose sex was never secret in spite of her pseudonym—

was a curiously paradoxical individual. Her full name of common usage was Mathilde-Marie-Georgina-Élisabeth de Peyrebrune (1841-1917), but she transformed her chosen forename in her signature in honor of George Sand. She was the illegitimate daughter of an English exile who claimed to be an aristocrat; her mother's surname was Judicis, but she adopted as her own surname a transfiguration of the name of her birthplace, the hamlet of Pierrebrune, in the Dordogne, occasionally adding in her father's surname (Johnston). At the age of eighteen she married Paul-Adrien Eimery, but never used his name after relocating to Paris following the catastrophe of the Franco-Prussian War of 1870. There she began writing for feminist periodicals and soon began writing fiction that eventually made her one of the most popular *feuilletonistes* of her era, serializing the novels that she produced in profusion in upmarket periodicals like the *Revue des Deux Mondes* and the *Revue Bleue,* as well as newspapers like *Le Journal* and *La Lanterne.*

Peyrebrune became an archetypal example of a successful "middlebrow writer," who combined great popularity with consummate respectability. In much the same way, she was one of the principal exemplars of a "respectable feminism" that took care to distance itself from the radical feminist movements that blossomed in the 1880s, following fierce disputes among the feminists of the 1870s between radical socialists—including Fourierists opposed to the "sexual property" of marriage—and *bourgeoise* reformers whose ambitions were far more moderate. "Une Décadente" is the most flamboyant move she made in that game of separation, presenting a caricature of one high-profile variety of radical feminism, which is demolished by the narrative in such an excessive fashion that it was evidently written tongue-in-cheek, although it is probable that some readers were oblivious to its sarcastic humor.

The narrative strategy in question is typical of her work, which routinely deploys an exaggerated sentimentalism, whose conventional rhetoric it scrupulously undermines with a satirical irony that is usually subtle but sometimes becomes corrosively acidic, as in "Les Fées," a cheerfully perverse parody of the watered-down second-hand *contes de fées* that Charles Perrault had standardized within the literary tradition. Although the two stories might seem quite different in their themes and narrative methods, they are both unrepentant Voltairean *contes philosophiques,* summarizing a challenge to conventional "wisdom," deftly and cleverly in the case if "Une Décadente," forthrightly and brutally in the case of "Les Fées."

"Une Décadente" is particularly interesting as a swift reaction to the repopularization of the label "decadent" in association with a perceived literary *avant garde* consisting of Naturalists and Symbolists (who were soon misdefined by critics as opposed schools). Initially deployed by hostile journalists as an insult, the "decadent" label was swiftly adopted by the more bellicose representatives of the *avant garde* as a provocative banner, especially after the publication of a parody of contemporary avant-gardism, *Les Déliquescences—poèmes décadents d'Adoré Floupette* (1885) by "Marius Tapora" (concocted by Henri Beauclair and Gabriel Vicaire), whose blithely parodic nature was unnoticed by the hostile journalists, some of whom fell for the hoax hook line and sinker. It was the success of that joke that led Léo Trézenik to title his 1886 collection of vignettes *Proses décadentes* (tr. as *Decadent Prose Pieces*), and prompted Madame de Peyrebrune to refer in "Une décadente" to "*décadents et deliquescents.*" Her novelette is, in essence, a straight-faced item of what Trézenik dubbed "*floupetterie.*"

The early 1880s was the heyday of the Parisian "Amazons," women who took satirical advantage of an old city statute that permitted them to apply to the Prefecture of Police for a permit to wear male attire in public. The political fashion statement had been made before, but the possibility of making it "official" when it was challenged was an attractive *floupetterie* of which several determined self-publicists took advantage. The fencing-schools of the city, running low on their traditional customers, had recently opened their doors wide to female clients, who flocked there in much the same spirit, compounding the scandal in the eyes of the popular press, which swiftly created a mythology of female duelists that was enthusiastically transplanted into fiction by writers proud to belong to the largely fictitious "decadent school," including Catulle Mendès.

Madame de Peyrebrune was in regular attendance at the literary salons and cafés where the alleged decadents hung out, and she was on friendly terms with most of them, including the already-notorious Rachilde (Marguerite d'Eymery), who was later to claim that she had only sported male attire in the early 1880s because she was hard up and it was cheaper. Although the story's Dr. Thiébaut does not include Rachilde in the list of *avant garde* writers he carefully excludes from stigmatization as morally and intellectually bankrupt, there is a sense in which the description of Hélione's eccentricities carefully leaves no room for her to be mistaken as a caricature of Rachilde—of which there might otherwise have been a danger, given that Rachilde had recently produced one of the archetypal "decadent" novels in *Monsieur Vénus* (1884), the heroine of which is an eccentric Amazon.[1] In fact, the predominant feature of Hélione's philosophy to which the narrative

---

1 Rachilde's friend Marie-Paul Courbe, who wore male attire and was an enthusiastic fencer, was at the center of the imaginary dueling scandal, and was thought by some observers to have been the model for the heroine of *Monsieur Vénus*, while others made the idiotic but all-too-commonplace assumption that the character must be a mirror image of the author. Rachilde certainly served as the principal model for the heroine of Courbe's own novel *La Vierge Réclame* [*The Advertised Virgin*] (1887; signed "G. de L'Estoc"), which was interpreted by some critics as a vicious tit-for-tat assault, although the two of them remained on speaking terms.

voice of "Une Décadente" takes exception is Nihilism, imported to Parisian salons and café society and made briefly fashionable there by a flood of Russian refugees following the assassination of Tsar Alexander II in 1881, its popularization aided by translations of literary works by Ivan Turgenev, who was fascinated and amused by the notion.

Peyrebrune was also well aware of the keen interest being taken in the notion of "decadence" in the clinical asylums of Paris, whose directors' weekend courses of open lectures were frequently attended by writers enthusiastic for insights into the vagaries of the human mind. The writers in question were inevitably interested in the idea, touted by several of the most vociferous alienists of the era, that all poets were mad and that "decadent" poets were the maddest of all. Most were enthusiastic to deny it, but a few, inevitably, were glad to lay claim to madness in a spirit of humorous perversity; Peyrebrune, in keeping with her own image, belonged to the former camp—unlike Trézenik, whose response is summarized in his novel *La Confession d'un fou* (1890; tr. as *The Confession of a Madman*). It is unsurprising that Peyrebrune employs physicians with a special interest in "mental illness" as the sympathetic male characters in her story, and that she approaches the "problem" of the heroine's ostentatious decadence by considering it as an illness in need of an ingenious cure. Being well aware that her own pose of conscientious conventional sanity was a mask for an authentic and intelligent sanity at odds in certain respects with convention, her intention was necessarily satirical.

Peyrebrune was inevitably bracketed in the eyes of many contemporary critics with "Gyp" (Sybille Riqueti de Mirabeau, Comtesse de Martel de Janville, 1849-1932), a similarly prolific pseudonymous novelist who published in some of the same periodicals, including the *Revue des Deux Mondes*, but Gyp was a much more strident character, politically affiliated to the far right, a virulent anti-semite who became a fervent anti-Dreyfusard. Although her fiction, which plowed the same sentimental furrow as Peyrebrune's thematically, was not devoid of humor, the undoubted seriousness and extremism of her opinions distanced her tone considerably from the lighter and far more moderate note sounded by her rival— whom Gyp, being an "authentic" aristocrat, doubtless regarded as a vulgar upstart.

As with many modern writers of "love stories," Peyrebrune's themes led to a sexist underestimation of her intelligence and ability, and the great majority of her works soon fell into a critical eclipse that persists until the present day. The stories in the present volume are atypical of her best-selling work, but they participate in the same deceptive cleverness, and although it would be stretching a point to regard "Une Décadente" as a homages to the section of the contemporary *avant garde* that it parodies she was by no means unsympathetic to the real ambitions, narrative strategies and rhetorical methods of those contemporary

Movements. She was perfectly capable of writing fiction in that vein herself; "L'Oiseau rouge" is an early example of a narrative strategy that became very popular among *avant garde* writers of the 1890s: symbolist accounts of exotic madness. "Salomé" is an archetypal decadent fantasy in a similar vein, published before Jean Lorrain and Remy de Gourmont produced their classic exemplars of that strange subgenre. There is no doubt that she could, had she wished, have gone on to make further contributions to the nascent movement. Although she relented after temporarily banishing Rachilde from her salon after the publication of *Monsieur Vénus* she apparently considered that it was not a direction she wanted to follow herself, and "Une décadente" can be regarded as a symbol of her own rejection of it, but "Salomé" remains a spectacular landmark work of decadent fantasy nevertheless.

✼

The translation of "Une Décadente" was made from the relevant volume of the *Revue Bleue* reproduced on the Blbliothèque Nationale's *gallica* website. The translation of "Les Fées" was made from the copy of *Giselle* reproduced on the same website. The translations of the other stories were made from the relevant issues of *L'Écho de Paris* contained in the gallica archive.

—Brian Stableford,
May & September 2020

A DECADENT WOMAN

Modernity[1]

---

1 The manner in which this subtitle is included in the *Revue Bleue* text suggests that it might well have been the author's original title, while "Une Décadente" was an editorial supplementation. "Modernité" is certainly a more apt title for the satire, but the emphasis of the newly-fashionable term "décadente" was probably considered as a selling-point by the editor of the periodical

I

THE celebrated painter of slightly eccentric feminine types with ideal and tormented lines, a disquieting expression, garments of violent color or very pale and harmoniously discreet—the mannered painter who had introduced japonism into modern painting[1]—had just completed a portrait of Mademoiselle Hélione d'Orval, and that daz-

---

1 The painter that the author has in mind is obviously Edgar Degas, with whom she was acquainted, whose pioneering Impressionist style was still considered rather shocking (and hence "decadent") by many commentators in the early 1880s. The name that Hélione eventually attributes to the artist is derived by means of a pun, substituting "voil" (a masculinization of a term for a veil) for "gas" (which can be seen as a modification of a French term for gauze).

zling portrait was now situated in the golden nimbus of its splendid frame in the center of a panel of the small Louis XVI drawing room annexed to the large apartments of Doctor Thiébaut.

Only the gold of the frame disrupted the harmony of the color of that room, all grays and white woodwork, for the painting melted into the general tone of the decoration with even more pallor and effacement. It was a delicate snowy fantasy in which misty tones faded away beneath vaporous blue hues iced with silver, like clouds against the nacreous white of a distant sky.

A young woman was standing, slightly stiffly, in the hieratic pleats of a silk as pearl-encrusted as a Byzantine fabric, bizarrely draped, falling and trailing, filling the entire bottom of the frame and seeming to prolong even further, beyond that snowy mass, the lunar light that veiled and dressed the standing woman like a symbol. In her ivory-hued hands with fine interlaced fingers she carried lilies regally. Her nacreous face stood out vaguely from the bright backcloth, scarcely tinted by an auroral pink and scarcely illuminated by the partly-closed somnolent eyes, disdainful and dreamy.

In the upper left corner of the frame, like a blazon, a horrible apocalyptic beast was twisting its deformed rump, darting out the silver arrow of its enormous tongue and suspending from its claws the crowned monogram of Hélione d'Orval.

"It's frightful," Dr. Thiébaut declared, frankly, whose wife was Hélione's younger sister and who had just entered in order to contemplate the new portrait. "Isn't that your opinion, Marcus?" he said, turning toward a young man who had stopped in the doorway, his gaze gripped and dazzled by that fantastic and celestial vision.

"No," Marcus replied, "it's merely strange. Perhaps it's even very beautiful. I don't judge, I sense, and my emotion is profound. Isn't that the criterion of great works?"

"Don't get carried away, my dear; your

emotion, in this instance, isn't addressed to the painter's work but to the model—confess it."

"Oh, I can only admit it," replied the young man, blushing, with a frank smile on his lips. "However . . ."

"However, as you've been maltreated by Hélione," the doctor interjected, "you won't be sorry to take advantage of this opportunity to pay court to her. For the portrait isn't so much the work of the painter as her own. It's her who imagined that profligacy of whiteness, the effacement of the hues, that garment whose form is copied from Byzantine stained-glass windows, the dragon and the lilies—because all of that enters into the formula of the artistic preferences of the group of decadents and deliquescents, advanced in the morbid sense of the term. And because she has turned her neurosis in that direction she's infatuated with the transcendent nihilism that a few young fools have made fashionable in the Latin Quarter, and which, I hope, won't pass over the bridges. We have quite enough of that on this side without also having its apology and its formula, which always complicate the evil. Oh, certainly we're decadent—but if we begin to take pleasure in it proudly, we'll be doomed. How many sick people one could save if we could leave them ignorant of their disease! Fortunately Messieurs the Decadents are almost all poets—which is to say, not dangerous from the viewpoint of the propagation of their theory, for, as soon as they express it in verse, no one hears them any longer."

"Hélione hears them, though," Marcus put in.

"Because she frequents a salon where the nucleus of the petty phalanx has its entry, and spouts its maxims gladly. In any case, they're playing decadence like a theorb in order to accompany their rigorously Parnassian poetry, of a form as clear as it is impeccable. They label themselves decadents in order to be noticed, and they preach decadence in order that people will listen to them, but fundamentally, it's a marvelous Renaissance that is in preparation, and which they're pursuing. They sculpt their verses as Benvenuto Cellini sculpted the gold of his flagons; they're artists. Besides which, they recommend to one another all the master smiths of golden verse: Baudelaire, Gautier, Leconte de Lisle, Catulle Mendès, Banville and Silvestre. And Laurent Tailhade, Stanislas de Guaita, Hérédia, Mallarmé, Verlaine, Jean Lorrain and others are clever disciples. Behind them, though, are the impotent and the spoiled who strive to be obscure in the hope of appearing sublime. Their pose, and their unhealthy dream, is to make night on earth and within souls. They insult the sun, the purple, bright flowers, health, life, woman and amour! *Nihil*: there is nothing. And that madcap Hélione, with her blonde hair and her divine beauty, repeats gravely, closing her eyes to the light: '*Nihil*: there is nothing.'"

"I despair," murmured Marcus.

"In truth, my dear, I don't know what to say to you. For two years you've been obstinate, with a veritably amorous patience, in trying to make the miraculous fount of amour spring forth from that closed heart, but you've scarcely succeeded, it seems to me, in making yourself tolerable to Hélione, who ordinarily cares little for scientists . . ."

"Oh, a scientist . . . !" Marcus protested.

"You're modest, my young master, but your works denounce you. If medical science takes a serious stride in our century, it will owe it to you."

"But really, colleague . . . !" the young man interjected.

"No; I'm a practitioner myself; I apply medicine; you're the bold theoretician who discovers in the marvelous compounds of modern chemistry the elements of cures, health and life. I profit from your discoveries; I apply your remedies, benefit from your results and collect the fruits of your labor, but the glory belongs to you and it will remain yours."

Marcus had turned toward the window, pensively, and was tapping the narrow pane in its leaden frame. Slowly, he replied: "As long as I haven't found a means of acting on the body by way of the mind, the art of curing will remain in the empirical domain. A well-constituted man would never fall ill if he possessed the instinct of the government of his body, like animals that never suffer and only die of wounds, accidents or old age. All medicine ought to be limited to repairing the stupidities that we commit every day against ourselves, as if we had made a decision to go against all the absolute necessities of our physical organization. The body would remain healthy under the direction of a sanely equilibrated mind. The equilibration of judgment, that's everything. So Hélione is visibly heading for a breakdown of her entire organism, perfect as it is, because of the nervous excitement that her overactive brain is communicating to her whole being. Neurosis, people say; not at all: mental breakdown, that's all."

"Yes, but try to cure her mind!" said Dr. Thiébaut. "Do you know a means?"

"Perhaps," Marcus replied, after a hesitation. "Nature is such a powerful auxiliary! And if you were willing to help me . . ."

"Of course! Can you doubt it?"

"Ah, but you don't know the means that it's necessary for me to employ."

"Whatever it is, it can't offer any peril for a woman you love and respect."

"Do you think so?" exclaimed Marcus, emotionally. "Well, preserve that confidence and try, under my direction, an interesting treatment. I believe I can answer for its success."

"I can count on it, then," the doctor replied, simply, holding out his hand. "Instruct me . . ."

But rapid footsteps sounded in the large drawing room, which it was necessary to traverse in order to arrive at the small one, and the door, violently thrown open, gave passage to Mademoiselle d'Orval.

She nodded her head, with a masculine gesture, and came to shake hands with the two men in a cavalier fashion. She had a grandeur about her in spite of the eccentricity of her costume: a black skirt, narrow and short; a tight black jacket open over a black satin waistcoat, over which dangled the somber end of a lace cravat into which a golden lily was pinned. Her hair, sternly put up, was heaped around her small and delicate round head, extending a golden blonde fringe over her forehead, cut straight above her eyebrows. She was very pale, her eyelids scarcely raised, her lip disdainful and her neck long, like the Venus de Milo. A sprig of white lilac flowered in her masculine buttonhole.

"Jacques," she said to her brother-in-law, "go and console Marguerite, who's turning into a fountain by dint of weeping for her son, who has toothache—in his future teeth, I assume."

"Not at all," replied the doctor, proudly. "José's first teeth came through yesterday."

"Apparently, he wants to exhibit the second batch," the young woman replied, "and that event is putting the whole house in distress;

one doesn't know where to take refuge."

She shrugged her shoulders and came to plant herself in front of her portrait, which she examined with a satisfied expression, her head tilted back and her eyes half-closed.

"A great painter, that Revoil," she said, speaking to herself in a voice that was hardly distinguishable. "It's said that he lacks line, but what need do we have of line? There is no line, any more than there is color; all is appearance, it's necessary to render appearance, that alone being real. The conventional real doesn't exist."

"However," Marcus put in, drawing nearer, "if the real, tangible, perfect model who posed for this painting didn't really exist, where would the painter have found that divine form, the exquisite beauty that 'appears' to us in that frame?"

"That beauty and that form would have appeared to him in another specimen, that's all," Hélione riposted, dryly, who did not like her theories to be disputed. "You're doubtless unaware that forms are only appearances and are modified in accordance with the eye that contemplates them, like colors."

"Are you quite sure?"

"There's no certainty."

"Everything is dubious, then?"

"Everything."

"Including the affirmations of science?"

"Science belies every day what it affirmed the day before."

"And amour?"

"Oh, my dear, let's not harp on about that; you're getting old."

"You don't believe in amour?" Marcus persisted.

Hélione did not even deign to respond. She moved her shoulders slightly, with a scornful expression, and turned round in order to return to the door; but, her brother-in-law no longer being there, she had to resign herself to keeping Marcus company.

Then, as if for the sake of bravado, she took

a golden case from her pocket that contained minuscule cigarettes, and prepared to smoke.

"You're harming yourself," Marcus said to her, rudely.

"Do you want one?" replied Hélione, holding out the case to him with a haughty smile.

"Thanks, but I don't smoke in the presence of a woman."

"Because . . . ?"

"It seems to me that the reason doesn't require demonstration, but if you insist, I'll tell you that it's a matter of propriety and respect."

"Respect for what? I don't understand."

"For her femininity, her delicacy," replied Marcus. "Respect for her tastes, which are generally of a nervous and refined sensibility . . ."

"Good," Hélione cut in, blowing a thin thread of blue-tinted smoke from her pale lips, which vaporized her features. "I understand that you abstain from that pleasure in the presence of a dowager or a young housewife of olden times—like my sister Marguerite, for example—but with me, it's an unnecessary privation; I'm not a woman . . ."

However, she coughed and had to throw her cigarette away, with a chagrined gesture.

"Mademoiselle Hélione," murmured Marcus, sadly, "in playing against your role in life, you're hastening toward a premature annihilation of your physical and mental being."

"So much the better," she said. "Since we're born to die, isn't it in the very spirit of the work of nature to do everything with a view to hastening that end, which is its goal?"

"It's nihilism that you're practicing in that?"

"Exactly; it's the philosophical theory of nations in decadence. We're a finished people, so let's hasten to disappear and make way for the races to come! Don't you see how the people around you are hurrying to live? All the discoveries of modern science have only one objective: to go faster. Time is being suppressed, engulfed, annihilated. It's a rapid, disorderly rush toward the end, in which the entire century is racing. That's why we're searching today for the quintessence of things, in order to have known, learned, accomplished and savored during the short duration of a life, everything that would require the duration of several successive existences to be brought to a conclusion. What good will it do me, then, to protect an existence fatally condemned to disappear, by depriving myself of living in accordance with my needs by the means of satisfying them that are multiplied every day? What does it matter if I only live for a day, if I can experience a world of new sensations in the course of that day? Hazard has made me a woman, but my will has made me a man; I have the double enjoyment of my form, my beauty, my virile intelligence and my liberty of thought and action. That isn't enough; I'm initiating myself in all the arts, especially the quintessential art of modern poetry, which can hold in a single sonnet all the impressions of form, color, music and perfume that charm to the point of ecstasy minds smitten with the ideal of beauty."

"Don't the poets you love proceed by elimination?" asked Marcus, interested.

"Yes, and above all by concentration. The last word of their artistry will be spoken by the one who will have found the formula for expressing in a single verse all forms, all beauty and all sensations. A single verse, perhaps a single word, like that of 'God,' which contains infinity and eternity within it. Then, as it will only require a second, the duration of a lightning-flash, in order to have 'seen,' by the light of that unique word, all the visible and the comprehensible components of the artistic unreal, to have embraced in time and space the fulgurant spectacle of all that is, has been and will be, the human mind, suddenly sated and devoid of desires, having attained the *summum* of human felicities—since it will have savored them all at the same time, which is the frenetic desire of its insatiability—the human mind will sink into the infinity of the void in a rapid fall, like that of a world extinguished in the bosom of the unfathomable cosmos . . .

"It's toward that end that we moderns are tending," Hélione continued, after a brief pause that Marcus' pensive alarm had not interrupted. "Do you understand now that the duration of life has no importance for me, and that you made me smile just now when you threatened me with an imminent breakdown? What does it matter? Even today, I shall have lived enough."

"You're twenty-five years old, Mademoiselle Hélione."

"Or twenty-five centuries," she replied, with a genuinely weary gesture.

"So be it," he said, "But do you really believe that you have learned everything about life, since you've never loved?"

"I know amour," she said. "That's sufficient for me. It's a banal sentiment, fugitive, naïve and conventional all at once, false, devoid of grandeur and incomplete, because it's human, almost always vulgar and low, perhaps necessary to societies in formation, but useless to peoples in decadence. We no longer have any need to deceive ourselves in order to toil, without too much disgust and ennui, in the continuation of the race. That race is finished; let's allow it to end without prolonging its agony; that would almost be a crime."

"However," said Marcus, stubbornly, "it would only require one hazard to overturn all your beautiful theories."

"What hazard?"

"That of an encounter, for example. Yes, if a young man were to be found in society who united in his person the rare and charming qualities necessary to please you, your heart . . ."

"I have no heart," Hélione interjected.

"Or, indeed . . ."

Another word occurred to Marcus, but stopped on his lips in confrontation with the candid boldness of the young woman, who was looking at him, waiting for the word uncomprehendingly.

She even repeated: "Or, indeed . . . ?"

"Indeed," he said, his head bowed.[1] Then, shaking his head to expel his thoughts, he went on: "Life is beautiful, however, in its naïve simplicity, in its sane and frank verity. They are closer to and more certain of happiness than you, Hélione, the women with calm brains who accomplish their destiny tranquilly. Created for duty, for love, for the family, for children, they find in that exercise of their innate faculties sources of emotion and joy that all your philosophical speculations and artistic deliria can never give you. By annihilating within you those precious feminine gifts, you are developing beyond measure latent faculties that will disrupt your cerebral equilibrium and make you a sick woman or a mad woman, forever unhappy. And when the years have

1 The subtlety of this exchange does not lend itself to translation. The *bien* in Marcus' "*Ou bien . . .*" [Or, indeed] has a markedly different inflection than the *Bien* that he adds subsequently, and no English word can reproduce an identical nexus of ambiguities.

passed, and you understand the negligibility and the puerility of your present preoccupations, and you see your life declining, which will not have brought you anything beautiful, good and consoling, a terror will come to you with a cruel regret—too late, alas! You will be completely lost, and you will grow old skeptical and hard, hateful and desperate . . ."

Hélione smiled, leaning her elbow cavalierly on the mantelpiece, her eyes raised toward the splendid portrait in which her mysterious beauty was enshrouded in lilial whiteness.

"Well, what about suicide?" she said, laughing wholeheartedly, provocative and beautiful, with that horrible word on her lips, curved for the triumphant challenge.

Marcus started. "One last word," he said. "I adore you. Hélione. When you no longer want your life, at whatever imminent or distant moment, be good for once, for pity's sake, and, as if you were giving alms to an unfortunate, instead of casting it into oblivion, give it to me. I'll thank you on my knees."

"There's my brother," she said, without replying.

As Marcus looked around, she slipped through a door and disappeared.

"It's up to us!" Marcus exclaimed, as soon as he perceived that he was alone with the doctor. "It's time."

II

WHEN Dr. Thiébaut had married Marguerite, Hélione's sister, the two young orphan sisters were living under the impotent guardianship of an old grandmother, an invalid who died shortly afterwards. Miss Holten, their English governess, remained with Hélione in the separate apartment in which the young woman resided, on the second floor of the elegant and comfortable little house in which the doctor had installed his young household and his consulting room, in the heart of new Paris, on the Boulevard Malesherbes.

However, in order to please Marguerite, the unique charm of the family life, who only seemed to live in order to adore the cherished individuals who surrounded her, Hélione took her meals with her sister and even kept her company willingly enough when Marguerite was not entirely absorbed by the cares and duties of her young maternity—in which case Hélione fled, with the scornful disdain of her Schopenhauerian philosophy.

She went then, followed, as if by her shadow, by the silent Holten, who was also a philosopher, but austere and mystical, having carved out a religion in the nebulous veil of spiritism and incessantly in communication with the most select spirits.[1] Hélione ran around literary salons, artists' studios, museums and libraries, taking a note here and making a sketch there, and further on a copy

---

1 Paris in the early 1880s was also in the grip of the Occult Revival, many of whose aspects became fashionable in society, including the "table-turning" fad that Americans dubbed "Spiritualism"; the French had to prefer "Spiritism" because an immediate transcription of the Anglo-American term already had a different meaning, pertaining to the Cartesian theory of a special "mental substance."

of an unpublished sonnet traced in red ink on illuminated parchment. She sculpted in one studio and perorated in another, learning and speaking the artistic jargon in which her mind, of real value, went astray and became unhinged. Having returned home, while Miss Holten, her hands placed solemnly on a three-legged table, resumed her mysterious colloquia with Dante and Shakespeare, Hélione had a bath and a shower, dressed for the *salle d'armes* and fired at the wall very skillfully, having no need of a master.

Afterwards, in order to relax, enclosed in her vast and somber chamber, devoid of feminine furniture, with stiff high-backed chairs, sculpted side-tables, panoplies, uncurtained windows and dead owls stuck to the beams of the black ceiling, Hélione, clad in a long black dress trimmed with ermine, with dangling sleeves, perched in a chair with an armoried and crowned back, her elbow on the table and her forehead in her hand, read some cabalistic work, some grimoire of alchemy, in order to help her commentate on Goethe's *Faust*, whose pages of bitter, deceptive and mystical philosophy she read and reread feverishly. That was because she was meditating a work on Goethe; she wanted to trace the chain of decadent poets back to him. She wanted to glorify him for having introduced pessimism into France, with the aid of *Faust* and *Werther*. It pleased her antipatriotism—a perfect sign of decadence—to show Goethe and Wagner at the two ends of the philosophico-artistic revolution that would cause an upheaval in France at the end of the nineteenth century, would change its esthetics and would stifle the antique, clear and bright French genius under the gray clouds and obscure artistic formulae of victorious Germanism.

It was not that Hélione was organized to become a writer or a poet: her mind had received no serious culture, and no vocation predisposed her to the métier or the sacerdocy of letters; very artistic as she imagined herself to be, she was ignorant of the art, science and arrangement of words that constitutes a style.

In spite of, and perhaps because of, these lacunae, Hélione was preparing to write a work of elevated philosophy as she would have undertaken a piece of embroidery on a screen, with no more suspicion of the magnitude of the work than of her own incapacity. She had yielded to the fatal pressure of an incomplete and false desire for emancipation that was throwing all the women of the younger generation out of the gynaeceum in pursuit of some kind of glory, celebrity or renown that would give them class—or, rather, declass them—by consecrating them as "artists." She also dreamed of effacing under that sexless qualification the divine sign of her glorious predestination to the role of lover, wife and mother for which she had been created. Finding those limits too narrow for her deflected ambition, she also worked mentally to destroy them. Proud of discovering sublime ideas and virile preoccupations, she believed in good faith that she was a strange and marvelous hybrid being, the first of her species, destined to be a leader of the crazy cohort of hallucinates, neurotics and lunatics of the *fin-de-siècle*, imposing on them her formula of quintessential art and her deceptive philosophy of a black pessimism and the label of "decadent."

Already, several chapters of Hélione's philosophical work had been sketched: a formless work that Miss Holten was striving to perfect and further to deform with the collaboration of her spiritist metaphysics. Every day, Miss Holten wrote under Hélione's dictation, for the duration of her inspiration. It was a pleasing spectacle, that of the two women, one of dazzling beauty, her forehead haloed by her crown of blonde hair, the other mature and grave, her gray tresses stuck to her matronly cheeks, enclosed in that large and somber study, where one searched for the silhouette of the pointed hat and long silver beard of some scholarly magician of the Middle Ages!

And bizarre words, crazily strung together by an incomplete science, burst forth in the silence, rising and seeming to immobilize by means of their cabalistic formulae the fearful flight of the owls nailed to the beams of the black ceiling. The panes of the round windows rejected the sunny daylight, which died away on the mosaic of the parquet in the pale florescence of decreasing tints.

Hélione was marching back and forth in her ermine-trimmed robe, her hands nervously crossed behind her slender waist, which was braced, her head raised and her gaze lost. She picked up a book and dictated a citation:

> *Emptiness and death! Annihilation weeps*
> *from everything distant:*
> *From the Earth to the black bosom of the*
> *soul of the uniform Wave*
> *Dolores weeps; and her tears rain*
> *Emptiness and death! Noble darts, and*
> *under the ire of the north,*

Holes, alas! Great Holes and heartbroken
  pools.
Pools and seas with immense tides
RISING: To you, Nihil! To the vanquisher
  of duration.
Glory to you, O killer without ease and
  without remorse!

Miss Holten, alarmed, raised her head.

"What is that, in fact?"

"It's suggestive poetry," Hélione replied, gravely.

"And . . . you understand it, Miss?"

The young woman made a superb gesture of her raised arm, from which a silken sleeve was hanging all the way to the floor. "It's sublime!" she said.

"I prefer *Hi ho, my darling,*" a mocking voice suddenly sang.

The two women turned around swiftly; it was Doctor Thiébaut, who had entered a moment ago and had been listening to them, murmuring: "Oh, the fools, the fools!"

But suddenly, his face straightened and he came to take Hélione's hand, seriously and anxiously.

"How are you this morning, dear child? Oh, those eyes! Were you suffering again last night?"

"No," stammered Hélione, slightly troubled.

"Don't lie, it's futile. Your face admits it. Come on, breathe . . ."

Gravely, he listened, his ear applied to the delicate chest. He became somber, and muttered something. Miss Holten had approached, very anxious.

"Is it possible?" she said, wringing her long, stiff hands. "Has the illness developed to that extent, and suddenly, without it being foreseen?"

"What tells you that it wasn't foreseen?" the doctor replied.

"But in that case . . . ?"

"Ah, you're going to criticize me, aren't you? You know how easy it is to bend that dear and foolish head to any government. Would anyone have listened to me if I'd cried: 'The danger is imminent, beware: cares, hygiene . . .' No, it required the danger to become manifest, suddenly, abruptly, surprising even me in order for me to assume an authority that has become a duty, and for me to impose the law of medicine upon this despairing invalid."

"What is this strange malady, then?" asked the heart-broken Miss Holden.

"Oh, the name is irrelevant," the doctor retorted, brusquely. "Come on, Hélione, Marguerite is expecting us for breakfast. Take my arm. Can you eat a little this morning?"

"I don't know," murmured the young woman, insouciantly. "What does it matter, anyway?"

"All right," he said leading her away, "I won't contest your ideas. It pleases you to let yourself die; that's your right, if not your duty. But it's mine to do everything to dispute so much youth, grace, beauty and future with 'the miserly Acheron, which does not release its prey.' For you'll never live again, foolish child, the beautiful life of which you're letting go. Never again, you hear, will your beautiful eyes see the sun, your beautiful lips touch the flavorsome perfume of a fruit or a flower. Never again will you be loved, adored, begged and implored like a divinity. Oh, life is good, whatever anyone says about it!"

"Is it in order to make me regret it that you're talking like that?" Hélione put in, a trifle bitterly. "In that case you're going about it the wrong way, my dear. It won't engage me to live to oblige me to consider life, for I find it absurd, myself, not to displease you, and so perfectly useless, even if there were nothing else, that I would give the few days that remain to me to know immediately who has given it to us, why, and with what objective. A sad gift, which I'll return without regret! Is it life only to be dying every day? Is it life to be limited in all our being, in our physical appetites, in the development of our moral and intellectual aspirations, in our miserable strength, and our derisory power of volition and action? We have just enough intelligence to understand all that we lack and to suffer therefrom, and just enough power to formulate desires that remain eternally unsatisfied. In order to content ourselves, in the narrow measure that is possible, we're condemned to create an ideal for ourselves, one for each exacerbated and insatiable need, and to pursue it relentlessly, while we have the certainty of never attaining it . . . that's life, though!"

"And here it is again," replied the doctor, moving away from the door to let Hélione into the warm and cheerful small drawing room, where Marguerite was waiting for them and the table was laid for breakfast.

The sun was blazing through the large windows with clear glass lined with pink; it was shining on the vigorous plants with which the corner was filled, rendered even brighter by the vivid coloration of spring flowers. It was sparkling in the crystal and splashing the whiteness of the satiny table-cloth, invading and warming the room, hung with blond and gilded leather. In that flowery sunlight, Marguerite, bare-headed, her brown hair hanging down, in a colorful state of undress, was laughing, slumped against the back of a comfortable chair, with her corsage open, where a semi-naked child was sprawled, his nose buried in the lace.

Behind Hélione, the doctor had exchanged a glance with his wife. Immediately, the hearty laughter ceased; Marguerite got up, heavily, embarrassed by a new and imminent maternity; and, suddenly saddened, she came to embrace her sister.

"How pale you are, darling! Alas, alas . . . !"

The young woman turned away.

"Come on, it's all right," cried the doctor, feigning brusquerie. "To table now; the consultation is over."

Meanwhile, Marguerite laid the baby down next to her in a large basket lined with blue satin; he was writhing, looking upwards, his cheerful eyes blinking, dazzled by the light, his little mouth open and chirping like a bird. And with the basket between her and the delighted father, she ate, with a burst of gaiety, quickly suppressed by the presence of the pale young woman who was going to die of a strange, mysterious and fatal illness—for that could be divined through the banalities of the conversation, incessantly brought back to that painful subject.

"Go on," said the doctor, suddenly tender. "Eat all that you please, my child."

And he sighed.

Then Hélione, putting aside the nourishing and healthy dishes, nibbled pickles or caviar on toast, a truffle, a bonbon with violent flavoring, or an insipid and perfumed preserve from the Orient.

Languid and distracted, she was scarcely moving, her gaze lost and her thought absent, flown in pursuit of some abstraction, while her delicate fingers, very slender, nervously caressed the electric fur of a young cat with cruel golden eyes: a true witch's cat, absolutely black and fateful: an almost sacred animal, in the shiny satin of its fur, like a nocturnal mantle for going to the sabbat. It was stretched out on Hélione's knees, rubbing itself voluptuously on the silky fabric with abrupt frissons, its loins extended and its claws drawn, its serpentine tail vibrant, ready to pounce, and abandoning itself, slack and soft, its eyelids bordered by a thin thread of ardent light.

That cat, very precious, had a decadent origin; the decadents venerated black cats in memory of Baudelaire:

> *Their fecund loins are full of magical*
> *sparks,*
> *And particles of gold, like a fine sand,*
> *Vaguely star their mystical eyes . . .*[1]

Hélione prided herself on a mysterious affinity with the black sphinx that haunted her abode and rubbed itself amorously on her hands, perfumed with enervating essences.

---

1 The final lines of "Les Chats," from *Les Fleurs du Mal*.

Marguerite suddenly stopped gazing at her son and extinguished the smile on her tender lips in order to say rapidly, with a deep frown:

"I'm dying of anxiety. It's necessary to put an end to it! I want, I demand, a serious consultation, within the rules. Certainly, I have every confidence in my husband, but anyone, on his own, can be mistaken. Two people can discuss it, and decide on a treatment. I'm going to call Marcus."

The doctor replied: "Marcus doesn't consult; you know that."

"He'll do it for us, for her. He loves her so much, the poor fellow."

Hélione shrugged her shoulders disdainfully

"You're pitiless," the young wife said to her. "Besides which, you're wrong. You wouldn't be ill, broken down and at the end of your vital force, as you are, if, like me, instead of enfevering yourself daily enlarging the circle of your artistic comprehensions, you'd followed the very straight and very simple path of true and sensate women: marriage and maternity. If you only knew how good, restful and pleasant it is to have no other speculations in mind than those that ought to aim at the wellbeing of the people one loves!"

"Happiness is just a word," replied Hélione, disdainfully.

"Fool!" cried the indignant Marguerite. Then, having looked fondly at her husband and her child, she calmed down. "Before denying happiness," she said, in a milder tone, "deny immediately that I exist!"

"That we exist," the doctor corrected, with a gentle smile.

"It's necessary to have killed in oneself all faculty of reasoning, or even of thinking, to find oneself happy in this Gehenna of a failed world," Hélione riposted.

"I protest!" Marguerite exclaimed. "Whatever you think, from the heights of your philosophy, I don't consider myself to be entirely stupid and I have the pretension of having some reasoning in this matter, only to talk about myself. Just like anyone else, I sometimes give myself the pleasure of arguing and thinking about the subject. I've envisaged the good and evil, the good and bad, of all human existence, and I've concluded, not like you, a pessimist, and not like the doctor, a fervent optimist, neither that everything is bad nor that everything is good, but that good and evil, being conditional products of life itself, are both disengaged, alternately, almost regularly, from the development of life, as a tree produces in turn leaves, flowers, fruits, the moss that corrodes it and the leprosy that covers it, wears it away and fells it. You only see the leprosy, the doctor only sees the flowers, but I see the fruit that produces the seed—which is to say, the germ of a new production, in other words, the continuation and eternity of life. And I think that it's beautiful enough to spend an instant on this earth and continue the eternal work there, not to be too sorry to have lived."

"Bravo, doctress!" cried the doctor expansively. "You nod assent prettily, it seems to me."

"You're producing naturalism without knowing it," Hélione deigned to respond.

"Oh, no labeling, I beg you, unless it's to found a school in the good sense of the word, in which case I'll enroll under its banner. But what is simple and true has no need of a formula or a flag."

"Art is true, though," pronounced Hélione, authoritatively.

"Eh! Nothing is more false, my dear. But it's the only falsity that I admit and that I practice."

Hélione made a mocking gesture of surprise. "You! And what art, if you please? Reveal that mystery to us."

"Mystery, you do well to say, for I'm forced, in order to explain my thinking, to unmask my batteries. Well, do you imagine that happiness, the happiness that you don't appreciate but which is no less precious for that, is so facile to conquer and maintain that it becomes banal and within the reach of everyone? Listen to me carefully—and you, doctor, plug your ears for love of me . . . No? So much the worse for you . . .

"But you don't know, then, unfortunate child, what great artistry it's necessary to deploy in order to construct, decorate and engarland this fragile edifice of happiness, how it needs a light hand, an alert mind, a lively, tender, passionate imagination, delicate taste, a healthy and frank poetry and an ever-wakeful invention? Oh, people think that happiness can be picked like a flower encountered by the roadside, by chance. Not at all. It takes a great deal of care for that rare and delicate flower to germinate, to grow, to blossom and subsequently to perfume your entire life! If so many people who complain of being unhappy had made half the effort, in order to acquire true happiness, that they wasted running after chimeras, there would be almost none but happy people on earth.

"But there you go; it's necessary to possess, with the science of life, the art of decorating and embellishing it. That's the true ideal, sane and, I dare say, sublime, if you'll be kind enough to permit it. And yet that art is false, for it consists of enveloping the worst miseries of our humanity with illusions. It consists of making ourselves believe that we can acquire and possess moral perfections that, in reality, are incompatible with the essential conditions of our physical organization. But that is pious, for it encourages us in the effort to arrive at those perfections, and the mere desire to possess them sometimes gives us enough virtue to appear to have attained them. That suffices for the happiness that we owe to others, as for that which we expect of them."

"That's not great art," pronounced Hélione, a trifle disdainfully. "Theologies had invented that before you, even more subtly and surely more poetically."

"But it seems to me," Marguerite riposted, very animated, "that they've produced enough fine artists; and I find it difficult not to appreciate as a great art the one that consists of kneading, modeling and fashioning a soul, in accordance with an ideal of justice and virtue. To sculpt that jewel and ornament it with precious qualities like precious stones—true ones or false, what does it matter?—to give it a mental beauty, a touching grace, to make a moral value and a model of relative perfection, isn't a work of manual labor but of artistry, and worth more than those Phidiases, Benvenutos and sculptors of modern sonnets, for example, whose special art—very precious, I agree—summarizes the whole formula of esthetics."

Hélione had risen to her feet, and Marguerite, who was blushing, gazed at her with a pretty challenge of her head, tipped back by the weight of her heavy hair.

"Let's not get annoyed," the doctor interjected, but with a vivid surprise in his joyful gaze. "And you, Madame, would you like to tell me in what corner of your wedding baggage you hid this manual of sage philosophy, so well hidden that I haven't perceived it until now?"

"That's because it wasn't there, Monsieur."

"Then you've acquired it recently? Tell me, I beg you, the name of the publisher."

"Don't you recognize his imprint?" replied Marguerite, whose fine and malicious gaze threw a discreet signal to her husband. "It was, however, before you that I made the purchase."

"Ah! Indeed, I now recognize the theories of Marcus."

Hélione interrupted the enervating caress of her clenched fingers in the black fur of the cat, with a gesture of surprise.

"Marcus! I thought he was only occupied with science!"

"One could believe that he isn't even occupied with that," replied Marguerite, "for he avoids talking about it in society. On the other hand, he's a brilliant talker about all the questions that are within the range of our mundane intelligence. When he comes here, as you never deign to do him the favor of listening to him, he falls back on me, and after he's told me his troubles, repeatedly, we philosophize on that subject and all the rest. Poor boy!"

"Again!" murmured Hélione getting up with the calculated slowness of her decadent grace. The black cat rolled to her feet, bounded and fled like a shadow.

"Yes, poor boy," repeated the doctor, "for nothing can cure him of his deadly love for you, and he'll go mad if . . . if you doom him."

Marguerite took her sister by her long floating sleeve as she went past her to go away.

"Tell me, for what do you reproach him? Isn't he handsome?"

"No."

"No!" cried Marguerite. "But he's an Apollo. A superb face, masculine, proud . . ."

"Brutal," finished Hélione. "Bushy all the way to the eyes . . ."

"With a gilded frizz," Marguerite finished in her turn. "The eyes . . ."

"Of a lion . . ." said Hélione

"An amorous lion," said the young wife.

"He lacks grace . . ."

"What!" cried the doctor. "He's not effeminate, spoiled, pomaded, like the stupid young men of your so-called artistic circles; he doesn't wear a necklace or bracelets under his garments, doesn't make himself up like a girl, doesn't intoxicate himself with morphine or hashish, and doesn't walk lazily with his eyes half-closed, swinging his hips. He's a man. But it's evident that that type of virile, strong, powerful beauty, full of health and life, can't please a young woman like you, who preaches the reversal of sex roles, dresses in masculine fashion, binds her delicate forms in vests and waistcoats, salutes with the neck, shakes hands brutally, fences with a sword, hunts, smokes cigarettes . . . that's evident, that's evident! You no longer need a master today, a leader or a support, you clever women, bold, artistic and decadent to excess. You no longer need a defender, you who kill with revolver in hand those who get in your way or wound you. You no longer need amour, that slavery of the true woman, nor children, that meek embarrassment of your arms, henceforth occupied in a virile manner. That's why you drive away Père Adam, degenerate Eves, and reserve your cold graces and smiles devoid of promise for the vile and impotent serpent . . ."

The doctor's voice had risen thunderously, but it suddenly broke off; the child, abruptly awakened and gripped by fear, had started to cry.

Now the doctor, curbed and on his knees, was rocking the basket anxiously in order to put the little one back to sleep, for it was time for his long midday siesta. Marguerite, leaning over her husband, her arm around his neck, watched the baby's moist and indecisive eyes close again, as he calmed down, with a smile. Silence fell.

Hélione remained there momentarily with her head turned toward the group, gazing at it uncomprehendingly, cold and bored. Then she turned round, opening the door with her lazy gesture, and disappeared.

III

DAYS had passed; spring had accomplished its promises and everything was reborn on the mild earth. The air was stirred by breaths full of life. Human sap spread out in rumors, rolling its torrential effluvia over the city from the sunlit morning to the evening, already vibrant with starlight.

One evening, Hélione was awake in the high and somber room in which her fantasy took pleasure. Quite alone, and vaguely occupied with the strange illness that was slowly but surely carrying her away, she had put on the marvelous dress in which she had had herself painted, dazzling white with a silken train, streaming with pearls. A strip of pearls crowned her, like an Oriental empress, above her loose blonde hair, a mantle of golden radiance. Her distracted hands were crushing orange flowers, enveloping her with an oppressive perfume. She was sitting in her armoried chair next to the high and round bay of a window framed by luminous panes of stained glass, the battens of which were open. The night was silvery, for the bright moon was enthroned in the depths of the sky, in her cortege of stars. A hallucinatory blue tint filled infinite space.

A muted rumor was rising all the way from the boulevard, where carriages were rolling and voices murmuring, Hélione was pensive, her head tilted back. So this was death? She was not in any pain, but her breathing was slightly oppressed at times, when she remembered that she was going to die. So what, since she did not regret it, and would not miss anything on earth? No, truly: nothing. Her sister, perhaps? But they were already separated by such an abyss! Anyway, it was necessary to finish one day or another. Well, she had lived. Would she live again? That was of no importance to her. And yet a brief frisson, a vague anguish, ran through her at the thought of the imminent and complete annihilation of everything that composed her being, grace, intelligence and beauty. She would have liked something to remain. But what? She did not know. A distinct emanation of her personality? A work? Yes, doubtless that was it: a work.

And, almost saddened, she looked toward the back of the somber room, only illuminated from above by a copper lantern perforated like lace. Over there, a shaded work lamp blurred the contours of a table on which it reposed, and the stern profile of Miss Holten, immobile, leaning on her elbows.

Hélione's voice rose up, slow and soft.

"Will the copy be finished soon, Holten?"

The Englishwoman started. "It's impossible, Miss; I've stopped; I no longer understand."

"What don't you understand, Holten?"

"Page 196, Miss, the entire beginning of the chapter entitled 'The Novel of the Future,' which begins: 'Events are insignificant, and always similar besides; intrigue is puerile, like a tale for children; only the movements of the soul are interesting. An entire novel can only express and develop the passionate sensations of a being gripped by the fact of its psychic manifestation, a manifestation that only has the duration of a day, a minute or an instant. Without accessory; the theory of milieux is false; the veritable milieu of a soul is its body, so it bears it within itself and transports it everywhere. Nothing has influence. The action of nature does not exist . . .'"

"Well?" interrogated Hélione, Miss Holten having fallen silent.

"Well, Miss, I've just finished copying the previous chapter, which contradicts this one on certain points: that of suggestion in art, where it said . . ."

"I know, Holten, I know. Accustom yourself to comprehending the subtleties of distinctions. Understand this: the idea alone is subjective. For example: a word expressing an idea or an impression awakes in me a world of other ideas and various impressions, whereas I contemplate the exterior and tangible world in vain, remaining cold, without a thought or a sensation. Do you understand? Anyway, copy without understanding, Holten; copy."

And, raising her calm gaze toward the divine clarity of the heavens, Hélione resumed shredding the perfumed flowers that strewed the floor all around her pearly dress, irradiated by the moonlight.

In her vague dream, however, she was beset by an ennui; she was fundamentally meek, and the struggle that she had been conducting for nearly a month left her a softened lassitude. The illness that she did not feel frightened everyone around her, and they were all suffering from it: her sister, her brother, and Marcus, it seemed, more than anyone. They were tormenting her to make her quit Paris, the air of which, it was said, was killing her. Thus far she had resisted, because, on the contrary, she could only live there, in full fever, in daily contact with all the intelligent seekers of both sexes, the excavators of rare and precious words, in a complete affinity of impressions with the abstractors of artistic and literary quintessence.

Her brain, accustomed to the most delicate refinements of fine and tenuous subtleties, all the way to the vanishing point of the idea itself, had acquired a sensibility of comprehension that acted in a rapid and intense fashion, as if all her cerebral forces were directed toward that end, to the detriment of her other, unexercised faculties.

In quitting Paris, she would be drawing away from the hearth where the sharpened subtle appetite of her thought could be alimented. It seemed to her that she would fall into a mental torpor comparable to the mental state of beings with a rudimentary encephalum; that thought frightened her more than death.

But finally, this evening, she had almost yielded and consented, no longer having the courage of the refusals that left so much annoyance around her. And there had been talk of an imminent departure for a cheerful estate in Touraine. She would depart, therefore; and a mild thought of sacrifice occupied her, like a desire more feminine than usual, to ornament herself, for those final days, with a grace of complaisance and submission. Without her being conscious of it, the certainty of soon quitting this life was already blunting the virile rudeness of her humor, so extraordinarily extended for years in the direction opposite to her veritable inclinations.

She was at that point in her meditation, which was finishing in internal ecstasy, in the most complete silence of the advanced night and the hypnotic light of the moon, whose face seemed to be leaning over her, when someone knocked on the large door striped and constellated by artistic ironwork.

"Who goes there?" demanded Miss Holten, in accordance with the formula, having already risen to her feet.

But Hélione, thinking of her sister, said to her rapidly: "Open it."

And Marcus came in.

"It's late," he said, "forgive me; but its absolutely imperative that I speak to Mademoiselle Hélione this evening. Where is she?"

Miss Holten moved aside, and the young man then had a sudden vision, like a magical tableau, in which, under a flood of resplendent light, in her brilliant costume of an Oriental princess, the white Hélione was crowned with pearls.

A surge of emotion stopped him, and when he walked toward her it was slowly, his gaze riveted, troubled and dazzled. Then, at close range, he said to her with a suppliant smile: "I'd like to kneel down to render homage to your sovereign beauty. May I?"

But she shook her head negatively.

He straightened up, gravely. "Doctor Thiébaut, whom I've just left, has given me the authorization—I might almost say the instruction—to come and see you this evening,

Mademoiselle Hélione, because it appears that you're leaving tomorrow . . ."

"Already!" she said, rising up in an abrupt revolt. Then, immediately, she fell back into her languid pose, murmuring: "What does it matter?"

"And the doctor," Marcus continued, "desires me to make sure that you are in a state to support the journey."

"But I'm neither better nor worse than I was a fortnight, a month or a year ago," she said, with a hint of impatience. "I'm not coughing . . ."[1]

---

1 Tuberculosis was endemic in Paris in the 1880s, greatly encouraged by industrial air pollution, while the sewer system and domestic water supply were still in the final phase of their completion. The disease was perversely Romanticized by some *avant-garde* writers, who found an exotic beauty in its wasting effects on poor young women, which were mimicked to some extent by the symptoms of "neurasthenia" frequent among upper-class young women. Tuberculosis inevitably became the favorite method by which writers of sentimental fiction would subject their young heroines to literary homicide in the interests of generating pathos and a sense of tragedy.

"Evidently," responded Marcus, in a low voice, as if speaking to himself. "Suffocation, subcontinuous fever . . . cyanosis resulting from the insufficiency of hematosis . . . acute tubercular asphyxia . . . very rare. Almost devoid of suffering."

"I don't want to suffer, Doctor," Hélione pronounced, dully. "And if the end has to be painful, I want . . . I request . . . that it be abridged."

"We're not there yet," stammered Marcus, turning his gaze away.

"Why lie to me? Do me the honor of telling me the whole truth, as you would tell a man. How many days do I have left to live?"

The young man contrived a weak smile.

"Many days, I hope, when you're cured . . ."

"Come on: you're treating me like a little girl scared of death. I'll prove to you that you're wrong to doubt my courage—or rather, my indifference."

"I don't doubt it," Marcus replied, "and I don't know whether I ought to feel sorry for you or admire the insouciance with which you admit the possibility of an imminent end."

"Feel sorry for me?"

"Certainly, for that proves that you haven't yet divined and understood all that life reserved for you—still reserves for you, let us hope—of happiness, and powerful, intoxicating, divine felicities! Will you permit me to tell you, Hélione, that your soul appears to me to be enclosed, like the little soul of a newborn child? What radiance can make it bloom, then, since all the flames of true love have not had that power? What shock can cause the envelope to burst in order that it might blossom, and finally drink from the sunlight of life all the healthy sensualities to which it has a right, and of which you're depriving it. One word, Hélione, and I ask it of you tremulously: have you never loved?"

"Never."

"Never has a fleeing trouble, a rapid frisson, agitated the divine marble of your body, on encountering a gaze that was seeking yours?"

"Never."

"You live, then, in the eternal solitude of the heart, devoid of dreams, devoid of hope, devoid of memory? And that solitude doesn't appear to you to be bitter?"

"Yes, sometimes," Hélione murmured, pensively.

"So?"

"Well," she said, nervously, "it's possible, in fact, that in the cerebral transformation that I've attempted to accomplish in myself, I've altered to a certain degree my native faculties, which prevents me from experiencing, like other people, sensations that are no longer within my reach. It's possible that the ideal of life is displaced in me, rendering me incapable of comprehending and wanting what I might have been able to attain, and desirous at the same time of another ideal, created by me, and inaccessible."

"What ideal?"

"I don't know. If I try to think about it, I get lost. However, yes, sometimes I search for something outside myself. For what? I don't know: something or someone that doesn't exist. I'm like an . . . incomplete being, displaced, outside natural law . . ."

"That's true," replied Marcus, emotionally. "But since your reasoning has remained so clear and your judgment so perfect, why do you persist in a path that you known to be false and devoid of a goal? You have the good fortune that your clear sight and your great intelligence might be able to save you. But how many women would be doomed, who cannot reason like you! For the present moment is dangerous for the intelligence, the morality and even the wellbeing of women. A wind of emancipation is blowing that is intoxicating them. The science that they are inculcating in a virile manner, which might be profitable to them in future, is, for the moment, too brutal and heavy for their delicate brains.

"This is an epoch of transition, evolution and transformation, which will lead more often to mental breakdown before having accomplished the imagined modification to the feminine type. Woe betide the weak! In this first intoxication, as in suddenly liberated peoples, women are getting carried away and turning against themselves the weapons abandoned to their frail, unpracticed hands. They are rushing toward everything forbidden to them, wanting to have everything, to know everything, to grasp everything. And they are ceasing to be women without having conquered the power of men, displaced, as you said just now, outside natural law, unable to feel any veritable joy or any complete happiness . . .

"But you, Hélione, you, so perfect and so sage in spite of your artistic infatuations, can you not stop on the fatal slope? Having gone astray, can you not return to the true path, meekly submissive to your destiny, resigned to the fatalities of your sex, and, ceasing to proffer all these negations that have amused your intelligence temporarily, can you not put your hands together like the beautiful virgins of Gothic missals and make a great leap of faith, hope and love?"

A frisson passed over Hélione's eyelids, which lowered in order to close and hide two tears that had suddenly sprung forth.

"What's the point," she said, after a moment, "since I'm going to die?"

"Who can tell? Perhaps life will return to you if you return to it; but it's necessary to want it."

She stammered, dreamily, her eyes now raised toward the dazzling infinity of light: "Love life! Resign oneself to its vulgar banality, perhaps to accept it to the point of desiring to live! That requires an initiation that I don't have time to accomplish. Bah . . . !

"What's the point, anyway?" she said, again, getting up as if to give him permission to leave.

Her gesture caused light to stream over her pearly dress and shifted the golden mantle of her outspread hair. She held out her hand to Marcus, perfumed to the fingertips by the crushed orange buds scattered around her, and which rained down over her skirt like petals stripped from a flower.

Marcus took Hélione's hand at the wrist, thus stopping the customary virile thrust; and while he held it imprisoned, he gazed at the dazzling young fay standing before him, utterly cold.

"Adieu, then," he said, his voice dying, "since you're leaving tomorrow. Adieu my dream, so long caressed, my hope, my life flown away, my happiness lost! One last time, hear this word: I love you!

"I love you, Hélione, understand that well, with an absolute, unique, eternal love. Whatever happens, I shall always remain faithful to you. Alive and far from me, or dead, I shall always belong to you. You will remain, even in the tomb, my ideal bride. I shall dream about you every day, thus associating you with my life in spite of you. In my silent ecstasies I shall see you, as if you were there, present, sometimes a young bride, all white, as at this moment, or a radiant mother sitting at my hearth, even more beautiful in your glorious maternity. I shall sit you down beside that blessed hearth as if on a throne, and I shall live at your knees, your hands in mine, your gaze on my bewildered gaze, and I shall always, always repeat to you:

"'Isn't life beautiful, my beloved, and how sweet our task is in this world, and what an incessant joy it is to accomplish one's work and one's duty, in the simple serenity of honest, pure hearts? Hasn't your soul become tender and accessible to the beauties of the earth, which you would regret not having loved in the splendid season of warm and vibrant summers, perfumed and intoxicated by sunlight, in the divine season of renewal when the heart palpitates and opens like a flower under the sap on radiant, rosy mornings still enveloped in the nacreous transparency of clouds, and in magically-illuminated nights, troubling and silent? Isn't it true that only having loved and having been adored, as I adore you, is worth the trouble of having lived . . . ?

"Now you can leave, Hélione; I shall keep you entire in my soul and in my memory, forever."

Then, leaning over the little hand, warm in his, he kissed it slowly, for a long time, until it quivered. Then, rapidly, he retreated into the shadow and disappeared. The heavy door creaked in its perforated ironwork. Hélione had not budged.

Suddenly, she had a long frisson and looked fearfully at the sky, which had darkened, the moon having been suddenly veiled. A strange sensation made her put her hands to her breast; she was stifling in that darkness, in that silence, in that abrupt solitude, as anguishing as if the door of a tomb had just closed upon her. Madly, she extended her arm, repelling the black void that was oppressing her. Then she uttered a shrill cry and let herself fall, stiffly, on to her chair.

Awakened by that terrifying cry from her customary torpor at the back of the obscure chamber, Miss Holten leapt up, ran, and started shouting as she lifted Hélione up: "Help! Help!"

But the young woman raised herself up again slowly, slightly distraught, as if emerging from a dream. Her sad, changed voice had unfamiliar inflexions when she murmured: "Shut up; don't call for help; it's nothing. A faint, no doubt. I suddenly thought that I was about to die, and . . ."

Hélione shivered again, and, like a fearful child, threw her supple arms around the aged Holten's neck, and concluded in a whisper:

"I was scared."

IV

DOCTOR THIÉBAUT owned a property in the beautiful land of Touraine, so pleasant and so healthy: Les Ormes, a sort of large farm with an old-style farmhouse. The fireplaces were vast enough to burn a whole oak tree, and the rooms large enough for the colossal feasts of the ancestors. A nice little wine, which one might swear could be mistaken for Vouvray—and was mistaken for it—was harvested from the surrounding vines, casked every year and aged in the peace of ironclad barrels, of which the cellar was full. Fields of fertile soil, sown with wheat, extended as far as the eye could see and the Loire, flowing between thickly wooded banks, formed a fresh and cheerful frame to the old habitation, dark and mossy, and very picturesque.

It was there that the doctor had brought his young wife on their wedding day, and they had almost forgotten it. Now they returned with Hélione, whom they had removed from the Parisian fever.

They had departed precipitately in the bustle of barely-packed trunks, and the hasty installation made a joyful din through the staircases and sonorous corridors, in which parcels were mistaken and dragged from one room to another with the laughter of the chambermaids, the carillon of little bells and the mad yapping of little dogs intoxicated by the fuss.

Miss Holten passed wildly from one room to another, carrying in her arms a three-legged side-table, from which she only wanted to be separated after having found a definitive and sure place for it; it was the familiar trickery of her spirits.

Hélione had shut herself in an immense room furnished in an antique style: a four-poster bed with camaïeu curtains, monumental old wardrobes bearing faded pier-glasses, in which one could still distinguish the pale pink of languorous shepherdesses and the celadon green of shepherds with pipes. Naïve and charming family portraits decorated the wood-paneled walls, worm-eaten and cracking. The little windows sunk in the thick wall opened directly westwards over the sunlit Loire, through the green lace of newly leafy trees. In the distance, everywhere, there were fields and meadows, tender or intense verdure, flowering hawthorn hedges, and trees snowy beneath their spring flowers; and a breeze scented by cut grass and fresh earth enveloped the young woman, motionless before that calm tableau.

What impressed her most of all was the almost mystical silence of the fields: that full silence, only troubled by the cry of a little bird and the buzzing of a solitary bee, in which the rumors of the brain calmed down and went to sleep—or, rather, fainted—allowing the lightened mind to float, with vague delights, as if fallen into the gray limbo of oblivion.

The first night that Hélione spent under the discolored curtains of the great ancestral bed was long and mild. She got up astonished, but not charmed, by the soft numbness of her entire being. As soon as the evening arrived, though, a violent ennui gripped her again, and she would have departed had it not been for Marguerite's tears.

The doctor had left them alone, promising to come back every week, and at the first appeal if Hélione showed any symptom more acute than lassitude or fever. If her condition became more serious, Marcus would come. In addition, he had prescribed walks in the open air, and mild distractions. Marguerite tormented herself in order to see that these prescriptions were followed. Alone, in her condition, she would not have been able to take the young invalid very far and very pleasantly, but she was aided by her entourage, the influence of which appeared to have been anticipated by the doctor.

In fact, a few days after her installation as Les Ormes, Marguerite having made her arrival known, all the inhabitants of the neighboring châteaux and habitations came running: provincial but charming families, whom she had met briefly during her first sojourn. She introduced Hélione and quietly put about a discreet and tender word. It needed nothing less to overcome the alarm that the sight of the young woman had initially provoked. Her attitude, her abrupt boyish gestures, her bizarre costumes and her language caused anxiety to the very correct and formal mothers, and intimidated the girls, who could not imagine that Hélione was a small creature like them, true missal angels with ingenuous and utterly innocent souls.

Charity prevailed, however, and no one thought any longer about anything but distracting the strange and beautiful invalid, and going for walks with her. That was not yet easy, for Hélione became horribly bored in such simple and candid company.

"Good God, what can one talk about to these brainless dolls?" she said to Marguerite. "I don't know their language, and mine plunges them into irritating stupefaction. I beg you rather to leave me in solitude."

But Marguerite insisted. "You'll see, when you're accustomed to it, that simple and honest common sense has its charms. Besides which, those little innocent souls are susceptible to great passions."

"I don't believe it."

"Study them. Sometimes there are passions that they don't know, and don't even know how to express. They're all the more interesting for that. In our Parisian society people expend a great deal of artistry and style in order to depict minuscule sentiments, passions that brush the skin or the mind. Here, where people don't know subtle words and savant phrases, they keep silent, but see how eloquent the confessions of beautiful naïve eyes are, and the sudden blushes of lovely candid faces. There are divinely tender little hearts under those dresses and high-necked blouses. Ignorant the provincial girls certainly are, but is that a bad thing? I don't believe so. Knowledge destroys faith, and I'm convinced that, in order to be happy, it's indispensable to believe in happiness. What means are there of being happy when one has made the discovery that happiness doesn't exist? And that dour observation is the bitter fruit of an excessively profound knowledge of life and being. I shall bring up my daughters provincially," Marguerite concluded.

What helped to persuade Hélione to allow herself to be taken on these beautiful group walks through the meadows and woods was encountering a young woman who was said to be a widow. Very sad, she participated with a meek resignation in the naïve games and excursions of the youth of the neighborhood. People paid little heed to her and if they talked about her it was with a certain mystery; there was a mourning in her life, perhaps a fault; no one knew, but it was known that she kept a broken amour in her heart.

Hélione drew closer to her, penetrated her intimacy, and, seeing that she was sad, hoped to find in that disillusioned mind a bitter echo of her own disdain for life. She was mistaken; the young woman was wounded, but she only cursed her own error and weakness. What she regretted was having failed in the goal of her entire existence, having rendered herself unworthy of the chaste and divine happiness of a nobly shared amour. She envied fervently the innocent girls who went forth laughing and holding hands with their future husbands, their foreheads crowned with lilies.

"Oh, if only one could begin life again!" she said, imploring heaven with an avid gaze.

Disappointed, Hélione then turned toward a poor girl, Mademoiselle Lucie, who taught the children of a rich family and accompanied them like a servant, in spite of her distinction, her youth and her grace. Stiffened in a grim attitude, unsmiling, she appeared to be the friend of whom she was in search. In spite of the proud defense that Lucie opposed to Hélione's flattering research, a familiarity was soon established between them, for they were both from good families, intelligent and educated as well as sad, willingly debating the causes and the effects of the miseries of this world.

One day, however, when they had lingered together behind the other groups, which were frolicking in the fields picking new cornflowers and poppies that had recently bloomed, the teacher suddenly burst into tears. Her rigid mask had relaxed; her face, now covered in tears, was illuminated by bewildered tenderness and passionate dolor.

"What's the matter?" Hélione asked her, surprised.

"Over there, him!" the young woman murmured. "He's going to forget me! Look, Mademoiselle, it's suffering too much to suffer alone, without lamenting. Oh, how lucky you are, you rich girls, who can choose whoever you please and marry someone who loves you. It's for us, poor disinherited girls, that life is hell. That beautiful life filled with devotion, amour, duties and divine sacrifices to all the dear beings who are yours, in hope and joy or tears—what does it matter?—but in which not one of your heartbeats is yours . . . that life, we see from afar, like a promised land that we can never enter, because we're poor and it's necessary to buy one's happiness down here. That young man you can see bending down, picking flowers with the others—for the others, alas—loves me; at least, he loved me; he would have liked to marry me; head clerk in a notary's office in the town, he wants to buy a charge, and he needs a dowry; he's looking for one. Oh, I'll die of it . . ."

"You'd be very happy, then, if you could marry him?" Hélione murmured, pensively.

"Happy! Oh, Heaven, all the joys and all the intoxications of life! Happy . . . ! But I love him, Mademoiselle; I love him . . . !"

Lucie's vibrant voice died away in a sob.

Suddenly, she raised her head, with a great gesture of surprise. What had she heard? Was it a dream, a hallucination? Whence came that tremulous voice that had murmured in her ear "You shall be his wife."

Hélione was drawing away at a rapid pace.

She had just thought that, being rich, she could give that poor stray the possibility of the happiness for which she yearned, if only to prove to her that her desires were illusory, a vain chimera.

Meanwhile, she passed through the long grass, brushing flowering herbs, under trees that were shedding their flowers like odorous snow in the joyous sunlight that was biting her shoulders—for she had no umbrella, that feminine plaything, but only a tall Tyrolean straw hat, from which her blonde tresses dangled.

She was slightly intoxicated by the pure air, her thoughts torpid, vaguely discontented by the "appearances" of gaiety, color, joy and life that surrounded her and seemed to be mounting an assault on her reasoned convictions. Certainly, by not going into things in depth, one could believe in happiness and have hope in it, perhaps desire it, but if one reflected on it . . .

Only, it was becoming extremely difficult to reflect and sharpen one's thought, to excite subtle reasoning in one's mind, in this absorbing environment, much more sensational and subjective than she had believed it to be previously. Something very material, very alive, but very pleasant, invaded you, which seemed to rise from the warm earth, from the germination of plants, from the electricity spread by all the beings scattered in great active nature: something obscure, but powerful, inexpressible but perfectly sensed and understood, as if the beings and things, saps, breaths and perfumes, were pushing you in the direction of their own activity, their movement and their life, toward a goal identical to theirs, fatal, inexorable and definite. It was like an enlacement in the vibrant chain of existence common to all organic beings, a recovery of possession by Mother Nature, a remembrance of primitive needs stifled by purely cerebral fictitious desires issued from the unhealthy exasperation of the nerves. It was like the diminution of a fever under the mollified circulation of refreshed blood, a penetrating health that brought into play all the regenerated physical forces.

"It's strange," Hélione murmured, with a voluptuous respiration of all those vivifying scents, "but it seems to me that I've never felt better. I truly believe that Marcus is right and that a miracle might be contrived if I began to love life . . ."

She passed even more slowly under the lacy green awning of the elms that surrounded the dwelling, curbed in a profound reverie that put an intense redness into her cheeks, pale for so long, while a slight oppression made her heart beat faster. She forgot herself in her first contemplation of that redoubtable and sacred nature, which suddenly awoke in her the obscure germ of she knew not what unfamiliar sensation, and new thoughts blossomed in her mind, impregnated by a vernal verdure. The charming round of the girls dancing in the distance, hand in hand with some timid swain, moved her gently. She began to understand, in seeing them all thus—the happy, the poor, the wounded, tending toward the same goal, aspiring to the same joys—that perhaps there was something real, true and serious in those naïve tendencies toward a perfectly human and, in sum, touching ideal—and perhaps even grandiose, since it had for an objective the glorification of that unknown and cruel power, life.

Hélione's esthetic philosophy was in the process of displacement, and an anxiety came to her, for her pride could not easily accommodate an error of judgment, and she reared up in a surge of willfulness in order to collect herself, to defend herself against the impressions that were assailing her and to recover the calm disdain of her superb nihilism.

With a bold, slightly feverish gesture, she broke a branch, of which she made a switch in order to decapitate plants with sweeps of her virile arms as she walked at a stiff pace along the path that brought her back to the house. But as she pushed the gate, abruptly, not fearing to injure her frail wrist, she stopped dead, her legs buckling and her breath suspended, and went very pale.

Standing on the perron, watching her approach, she had perceived Marcus.

V

NOW, an animation rendered the old house with the sonorous wood paneling noisy from morning till evening. New guests had been installed there. Firstly there was Marcus, very grave, and then the doctor, as if he feared the approach of a fatal crisis. Finally, there was the poor young teacher devoid of a family, whom Hélione had welcomed in order that she could prepare for her wedding in possession of herself and the thoughtful idleness that renders the expectation of fiancées so pleasant.

Then again, there was a Breton nurse who sang incessantly the tra-la-las of her future cradle-songs while awaiting Marguerite's new baby. Miss Holten having consulted

Shakespeare, the table had replied to her that the child would be a girl. And people joked about that, although with sudden reticences, for Hélione had requested that the newborn should be given her name, and everyone seemed to fear that the beautiful godmother might not witness the baptism.

That dread appeared evident to Hélione, precisely because everyone affected to persuade her that she would be there. They really put too much insistence into it. How could they not comprehend that the presence of Marcus, who scarcely quit her, and the doctor, who followed her with his eyes with an anxious persistence, had informed her of the imminent catastrophe? She knew that these bizarre maladies hardly every forgive; one day, a sudden asphyxiation would grip her, and then . . .

But she put an obstinate pride into not seeming touched, and her haughty soul defended itself against the assault of natural weaknesses.

Meanwhile, recently, she had been suffering; her heartbeat had become more rapid; a thinness was elongating her delicate features, and a shadow was traced beneath her lovely golden eyes. Valiantly, however, she denied her insomnias, and even affected a mocking gaiety and almost coquettish graces. It pleased her to make herself adored and regretted.

Now she dressed, like the provincial girls, in bright fabrics, very virginal and very feminine, and one saw little bunches of florets, like confessions, at her corsage and in her hair. She greeted people politely, very daintily, with beautiful slow and mocking reverences, which rendered her adorable. Her gestures were supple and seductive; she amused herself by seeming as fearful as a little girl and trailing along indolently on the arm of young men with whom she went for walks. It diverted her to sense that she was seductive enough to drive someone crazy and to see Marcus going pale when she looked at him at some length, her eyelids fluttering, like a naïve but intimidated little schoolgirl. The game pleased her; she even allowed herself to be drawn into it, and it sometimes happened that she was shaken by an abrupt frisson at the sudden thought of the illness that was carrying her off and would steal her away from that jolly fashion of living, so mild and languid.

Subsequently, she was seized by an extraordinary passion for Lucie's happiness, which was her work. She had provided the dowry and the trousseau; she wanted to work with her hands on the bridal costume, which a squadron of seamstresses had come to the house to confect. In the large room where they were sewing, there was an orgy of whiteness on all the furniture; clouds of muslin and gauze buried the cheerful young laborers, who sang.

Lucie, still trembling at her overwhelming good fortune, incessantly paraded through the house eyes brilliant with joy and tears, gauche and bewildered in the midst of all those splendors, which were for her, and all the hasty toil that was preparing her triumphal wedding-feast. She could have kissed the hem of her benefactress' dress when the latter, crossing the courtyard, repeated: "Quickly, quickly; let's get a move on; the myrtles are in flower, the groom is waiting . . ."

They were also working, in a corner, on another tiny trousseau and a little couchette as large as a jewel-case, all in lace. Little beribboned bonnets crowned Marguerite's fist and the doctor's index finger by turns; child's vests starred with their bright batiste the bride's trailing skirts. The nuptial veil enveloped the cradle. That juxtaposition troubled hearts. The fiancés dared not look at one another. Marcus fled. Hélione, very pale, forced herself to smile.

And every evening, when the sun set, the day's work being concluded and the seamstresses having departed, the whole family and their guests descended to the base of the perron, into the freshness of the trees and the lawn, florid with large crimson baskets. They sat down, turned toward the sunset, moved by an instinctive need to follow the light that makes flower-heads swerve; and the dreamy conversation languished in the exquisite peace and somnolence of the evening. In the distance, at the far end of the avenue of elms, the Loire sparkled beneath the redness of the sky. The fields dressed themselves in shadow, and the chirping of the birds died away over the finishing rhythm of a hymn chanted in the distance.

The month of June has arrived; the seduction of Nature is complete; she now has all her strength, all her power and all her beauty. Here she is, victorious, Venus Genetrix, the fecund mother with teats streaming with the effluvia of life. In breathing, one inhales and one shudders. Saps are spreading everywhere, the flowers broadening their cups, into which the sunlight is falling and igniting incense; fruits are bursting and their aromatic pulp is summoning the swarm of pecking birds and golden bees, which will sow in the air a subtle appetency of fresh perfumes.

The earth is fuming, warmed by its subterranean transformations and mysterious combustions, which absorb death and throw life back to us. The furrows have germinated; the blonde wheat is already flourishing the delicate odor of ground flour, nourishing and healthy. Over the scythed meadows, the dying herbs exhale the chromatic scale of their mingled scents, as intoxicating as a liqueur. A rain of invisible sparks seems to be flowing through the blazing air all day long, peppering the epidermis, which drinks it and shivers.

A slow ecstasy unites and confounds the whole immobile body and the great soulless being of unconscious, mute and divine Nature; and in the marvelous silence of that grandiose infinity, the winged turbulence of painful petty thoughts takes fright, falls and dies. Then instinct, liberated from its chains, rears up, stretches, grows, rises and, opening its arms, face to face with the giant mother with the fecund loins, Nature, her forehead crowned with stars, it takes her, embraces her and glues its famished lips to the powerful bosom that pours the floods of life into it.

The month of June has arrived, and Lucie's wedding is imminent, so imminent that the fiancés, already ideally wed, display their happiness naively, with the audacious innocence of pure hearts. Sitting next to one another, hand in hand, eye to eye, they incessantly exchange the same embrace and the same smile in the serenity of a hope of inexhaustible delights. They do not see anything around them, as if nothing existed beyond themselves.

Meanwhile, close by, under the same foliage, Marguerite is rocking her son; the doctor, sitting at her feet, is playing with her unbound hair. Hélione, tilted back in her chair, paler, her eyes half-closed, seems to want to conceal her thoughts. Marcus, leaning back facing the setting sun, is contemplating her with a bewildered dolor.

Rare words punctuate the calm silence of the evening with long moments of silence. The fresh wind babbles in the foliage; sleeping birds whimper in their dreams. The occident pales; the Loire extinguishes its blue clarity rippled with pink; night approaches, dragging its first stars and its thin golden crescent.

Slowly, the fiancés have risen to their feet, their arms enlaced; they walk, so united that their footsteps have the same harmony, the same languid and lazy rhythm. They go along a path that turns toward the fields, as if they were walking into the mysterious night. Their shadow fades away. The doctor leans toward his wife, smiling, speaks to her in a low voice and kisses her silently

At that moment, Hélione's raised eyes fill with a sudden clarity, as if long-suppressed tears had finally surged forth. Abruptly, she gets up, her footsteps fleeing, and runs straight ahead, along the avenue of elms ending at the river, toward the last glimmers of the vanished sun. So rapid is her course that Marguerite only perceives her when she is already distant, out of voice range. She stands up and tries to follow her, trembling with an inexplicable anguish; but her husband holds her back and, making a sign to Marcus, says to him:

"The time has come. Go."

Then, while the young man launched forth by way of a covered path that would intersect the route that Hélione was following, the doctor seized his wife in his arms and began to weep with her in the anxiety of that supreme moment, so long anticipated.

Hélione was moving with an automatic tread, as if she were walking in a dream, her eyes wide open, her face streaming with hot tears like a rainstorm. Rapidly, she arrived at the edge of the river, which was ferrying sheets of radiance with a slight sound of splashing eddies, soft and regular. Quite alone, she let herself fall on to the shady bank, her face in her hands. She wept like a child, her sobs singing plaintively, punctuated by heavy sighs. It seemed that she had to empty her heart of chagrins that had been suppressed for a long, long time.

Finally, she straightened up, blinded by the tangle of her loose blonde hair, parting it furiously with her small fists, murmuring brief words. Suddenly, she uttered a cry, bounding to her feet; she had just perceived Marcus standing beside her, extending his arms as if to sustain her.

Immobile and expressionless at first, her gaze fixed, searching for her thoughts, no longer breathing, she suddenly flexed, with a great frisson of her entire body, and came to collapse on Marcus' shoulder, crying through her sobs:

"Ah! Save me, save me! I want to live!"

Then, when that word had finally emerged from her lips, she no longer stopped. "Do you hear me, Marcus?" she repeated, breathlessly. "I want to live! I'm young; I haven't lived; I don't want to die; I want . . . I want my share of happiness, my share of sunlight and joy . . . I was mad; I lied; take pity on me; save me, if you love me . . . for you do love me, don't you? And you won't let me be taken away by death?"

He tried to interrupt, but she struggled.

"No, no! Listen to me look at me . . . wouldn't it suit me, the white dress of a bride? Wouldn't my hair be beautiful under a nuptial crown? Tell me Marcus, wouldn't you like, if I lived, to sit down at my knees and kiss my hands? Oh, these happy people that surround me, they're killing me! That Lucie, radiant, full of life! Marguerite, with her children! Her children! Oh, Heaven! But I have entrails too, and I want, I want . . ."

She choked, seized by a delirium, which made her crimson and transfigured her in the sheet of gold that drowned her tilted head, gazing up at the sky, imploring.

"You'll live, then, Hélione," pronounced the trembling and broken voice of Marcus. "You'll live, since you love life."

"It's you I love," murmured the young woman, as if asleep now, her eyes closed. "But the malady that I have here . . . ?"

She touched her heart.

"I repeat to you that you're saved, for you were ill in the mind, not the body."

She straightened up and, drawing apart rapidly, said: "What are you saying?"

"It's necessary to forgive us, Hélione; we've deceived you. You detested life; it was necessary to make you love it, and for that, to persuade you that you were going to lose it. . ."

Hélione passed her hand over her forehead, and then took a deep breath.

"I understand," she murmured. "I understand now . . . I wasn't ill, then? I'm going to live, aren't I? Live! You're quite sure?"

And her gaze lit up and ran around her, touching everything, retaking possession of everything she had believed lost. She respired all the scattered life, drinking the air with an avid palpitation of her smiling lips. She was reborn, and blossomed in an expression of new and triumphant beauty. She came upright, like a flower on its stem; she appeared magnified and fully-developed. Her blood flooded her cheeks. She was, it seemed, miraculously born, a sudden issue of the powerful vegetation that enveloped her and in which her delicate nymph-like feet were still drowned. And she listened to the sound of that sap rising within her, invading her and shaking her with frissons.

Marcus was alarmed by her silence.

"Can you forgive me?" he whispered, trembling.

Then, abruptly, Hélione burst into mad laughter, staccato, nervous, prolonged and inextinguishable, which was that of overflowing joy. That bright, vibrant laughter sounded a fanfare. It awoke the birds in the foliage and the echoes of the bank. A tumult of laughter ran around her and then died away. Hélione had suddenly become tender as she looked at Marcus.

"Forgive you?" she said, finally. "Forgive you, when I'm searching for a word to express to you all the gratitude that I feel, and . . ."

"Don't search," Marcus interjected, swiftly, his knees flexing before her, "but give me your hand."

"Here it is . . . my fiancé," she added, in a whisper while he kissed, for the first time, the tips of Hélione's divine fingers.

And as night had almost fallen, they took the path to the house again, along the avenue of elms, their arms enlaced too, at a similar rhythmic pace slow and pensive beneath the first stars.

It was thus that they arrived at the lawn, from which Marguerite and her husband, wearied by emotion, watched them coming. As they drew closer, though, Hélione blushed, without daring to undo the enlacement that admitted and revealed her engagement to Marcus. She lowered her eyes, so modestly troubled that Marguerite, frightened and still tremulous, no longer recognized her.

"Hélione! Hélione!" she stammered.

Then the young woman detached herself rapidly, ran to her and embraced her, without speaking.

And while the two men, violently moved, shook hands vigorously, Marguerite murmured in her sister's ear: "Well . . . ?" Then, wanting to lighten the mood, she immediately added: "And the decadent woman?"

"The decadent woman has had her day," Hélione replied, in the same tone, "her time and her work, from which the Renaissance has emerged, as from a tomb."

"Mademoiselle!" cried Miss Holten. She arrived with long English strides, waving a voluminous package in the air.

"What's that, Holten?"

"It's the proofs of Mademoiselle's first volume, which have finally arrived."

"Ah!" Hélione replied, gaily, with a comical gravity. "That's serious. Give it to me quickly, Holten, hand it over."

Then, with a petulant gesture, she took possession of the package, twisted it sharply and shook it in the air, shouting: "Kin Kin!"

The dog, which was asleep, bounded to its feet in a storm of shrill yapping.

"Catch, darling!"

The packet pirouetted in mid-air and fell on to the grass with the dog, which ripped it to pieces.

"There they are, corrected," said Hélione, tranquilly. "Let's not mention it again."

"Bravo!" cried the doctor. "Philosophy is vanquished by amour!"

"Not at all," riposted Hélione, smiling maliciously. "The thesis has merely been modified; for a little philosophy doesn't spoil matters of amour. Just ask Marguerite."

"Certainly," the young wife replied, "but a healthy and cheerful philosophy . . ."

"Optimism, then?" pronounced the doctor, triumphantly "Hurrah for . . ."

"Stop!" Marguerite interjected, swiftly. "Optimism is the philosophy of egotists, just as pessimism is the philosophy of the unhappy. To have the objective of searching for one's happiness by working for that of others is the veritable philosophy of honest people, which only lacks a name. Baptize it, Marcus."

"It's done," replied the young man. "You've named positivism,[1] a philosophy that is in disfavor today."

"For what is it reproached?"

"For being sensate."

"It's dead, then!" exclaimed the doctor, in jest. Then he turned to Hélione. "And there you are, dispossessed, my beautiful theoretician: no more label, no more flag, no more dogma . . ."

"Well, what about this?" said Marguerite, emotionally, presenting her son. "Isn't the philosophy of woman, her religion, her faith and her safeguard, maternity?" She drew her-

---

1 This seems odd nowadays, when the label of "positivism" is applied exclusively in the context of the scientific dictum that only statements that can be proven by empirical observation can be admitted as true (leading to endless quibbling about the extremism of the relevant standards of proof), but Auguste Comte, the promoter of positivism, also used it for the title of a secular religion based on the dictum *vivre pour autrui* [live for others], the basis of the moral philosophy whose name was translated into English as altruism.

self up to her full height, splendid and august in the sacred deformity of her womb.

"You're right," murmured Hélione, having become serious again. And, holding out her arms, she took possession—which she had never done before—of Marguerite's little child. Then, drawing away slightly, awkward beneath that light burden, she went to sit down alone at the end of a bench in a gap between the trees. The bright light of the sky allowed the sight of all the frail grace of the pink and delicate little being, so tender and so timid, that little parcel of milky flesh, almost formless, which was a person and which would become a man.

She contemplated him, curiously, attentively and thoughtfully. Then, slowly, she drew him toward her and wrapped her arms around him, with the divinely tender gaucherie of a Raphael virgin.

Marcus, respecting that touching initiation into the sublime role of mother, remained at a distance, but his heart was prostrated in an infinite adoration to the feet of the celestial vision, in which nothing was lacking, neither the white robe of the Virgin, nor her radiant beauty, nor the golden nimbus of her floating hair, not even the backcloth of the sky, scintillating with stars, which crowned her.

THE FAYS

THERE was once . . . a king and a queen. It was in the remote times when there were true kings and veritable queens—which is to say, those mysterious and almost super-human elite beings whose quasi-divine origin is lost in the darkness of the centuries and who, on the redoubtable foundation of their royal ancestry, governed their peoples without ever having seen them and without the latter ever having contemplated their august and sacred faces.

Enclosed in the triple enclosures of the gigantic walls of their giant palaces, built on the summits of hills and puncturing the skies with their gilded cones, like spearheads, while the tall pilasters of enormous porticos seemed to lift up the white curtain of the clouds, those kings—the only ones worthy of the title—lived and died in the eternal monotony of their Olympus without ever quitting it, except, clad in iron masks, for distant wars. And they maintained thus, with a proud sanctity, the ancient and hieratic majesty of their ancestors.

When fêtes or tourneys summoned princes and peoples to the vicinity of the ramparts of the palace, the doors only let out the small society of servants and minor functionaries. The remainder showed themselves above the granite of the walls and the dazzling marble of lofty terraces surrounding the ivory tower, perforated like a Byzantine campanile and erected on the top of pilasters, which enclosed, in its niche of golden cloth and the constellation of gems that shone thereon, the slender and completely invisible majesty of the veiled queen.

And, on scarcely glimpsing her, like a star at the zenith, the kneeling people shivered in fear.

Thus kings ought to reign.

However, human life unfolded for the very powerful princes of the realm of Evir with the joys and terrors common to all mortals; for neither the shiny bronze of heavy closed doors, nor even the grim gods engraved and painted on the flanks of propylaea, arrested the inevitably entry of the miseries of existence, and the subtle breath of bewildered passions passed over the ramparts victoriously.

If, from the redoubtable vision of vast palaces and their giant walls enclosing mysterious cities of a sort, one crossed the enclosures, the ditches and the towers, traversing the quadrilaterals of courtyards paved with gleaming mosaics, one reached, miraculously, the jasper portico guarding the intimate threshold of the quasi-tabernacle in the depths of which their royal majesties lodged and if, provided with a charge that permitted parting the formidable and sacred curtain behind which kings live and sleep, the frightened eye were able to contemplate their faces, this is what it would see:

First of all, very small as if lost in the immensity of halls hung with crimson and gold, a dainty little girl, tall and pale, with long hair falling in blonde tresses, the naïve face of a Gothic virgin, sitting stiffly in her bright robe embroidered with sunflowers and fringed with topazes. The pectoral of her royal tunic resembles a golden breastplate. Also gold are her cathedra, raised up at the top of numerous steps, and the awning that covers it. That resplendent throne is situated under the arch of an ogival bay open to a sky gilded by the fires of the sunset, and behind it is displayed the distant vision of horizons lost in an immense desert, which unfurls the dazzling brightness of its golden dust endlessly.

That little girl, similar to the virgins of a missal, is the queen, and she has just given birth. However, her gaze is sad and her mouth has a crease of mute distress. And beneath her long and gaudy pearl-encrusted dress, the bird of paradise that God has placed in that frail cage—her heart—is beating violently. It is palpitating, that gentle, wounded heart, for close by, leaning his elbow on her chair, tall and proud, stands the king, who does not love the dainty and beautiful queen, even though she has just given birth. He married her, in accordance with the prevailing custom, by virtue of a treaty of war, while the bride was still in her cradle.

When she was taken to him, scarcely nubile, he found her to be not to his liking, and neglected her shortly thereafter. He abandoned her to the duennas and the eunuchs, in order that she would be well-guarded, only allowing her—a child herself but a queen nevertheless—to watch children playing, pages and damsels who cheered up the solemn silences of the great palace of Evir with their irrepressible frolics.

So, sitting all day long in her high cathedra and lost in the stiff brocade of her enormous dress, the neglected little bride remained pensive and sad, with occasional sudden bursts of pretty laughter when some page took pleasure in diverting her in order to pay his court. One of them, moved to pity, knew the best ways of distracting her. He only appeared to live in order to serve her passionately. She looked on him kindly. And who could blame her? The little queen sometimes, while thinking of him, went to sleep consoled.

The powerful king was unhappy himself. Yes, possessing everything, he was miserable, for he could not obtain the amour of a haughty princess who lived at his court.

Tall, proud and bold, riding her hackney with the audacity of a heroine, with the commanding gesture and the imperious disdain that befits queens, the latter seemed to the king to be much more suited to sit by his side than the frail and timid child that fate had imposed on him.

And see how well he reasoned, for the young page who loved the queen so much thought the same, agreeing that things would have turned out more logically if the lady of the court had been paraded on the golden throne, while the blonde little girl who reigned wearily had come to play games with him, and belonged to him, in all honor, as a wife.

The queen thought, for herself—silently, unable to say so—that not being loved by a king is perhaps a lesser evil than that of loving a handsome page. And her heart, poor bird, sometimes languished in mortal dolors and sometimes beat its golden cage urgently.

So, on the day when the king was leaning a nonchalant elbow on the throne where the queen was sitting palely, there were noisy celebrations throughout the realm of Evir. The crowd was pressing on the granite walls around the palace and its voice rose all the way to the summit of the terraces like the rumor of the ocean. At the four points of the horizon the brass of trumpets sounded alternately. The entire city resonated to the silvery din of cymbals, while bells rung at full tilt howled through all their bronze mouths.

And the crowd, with eddies like waves, brayed endlessly the name of the kings of Evir;

for a prince had been born, the first of the young royal couple, and thus would be continued the dynasty of that ancient race, whose origin was lost in the darkness of the centuries, like that of the gods. Sure at least of still having a master whom it would be glorious to obey, the wise Evirean nation delivered itself to joy in acclaiming its prince and blessing the heavens. In addition, the king had been doubly liberal, for a son had not arrived alone, but accompanied, like a twin flower, by another fragile and delicate body, of a daughter.

Whereas the little prince was dark in his complexion and his eyes, and even the down on his little head, the unanticipated little princess was as blonde and pink as the dawn, for which reason she was named Aurore. Her birth had extracted a smile from the discolored lips of the poor martyrized mother. She thought that if the king took her robust son away from her, he would surely leave her the paltry girl, as one leaves a doll in the hands of a child; and her reverie was already adorning her with amorous graces. Oh, if she, at least, could one day be happy!

She obtained from the king—tenderly inclined toward her momentarily—that in order to ensure the future happiness of the infanta, all the fays of the mythical religion of Evir would be invited to her baptism.

The king did not believe in the myths with which antique faith governed the souls of his people, but he lent himself gravely to the religious practices informed by tradition, and the priests who guarded the secret of words and evocative magic formulae were protected by him with marks of profound veneration. So, having granted the queen's wish he summoned the mages; the latter invited in their turn sorcerers, conjurers, fakirs, Brahmins, spiritist mediums and evocateurs from the depths of India, Egypt and Syria; and the order was given to prepare for the magical enchantments.

The queen had not asked for anything for the young king, so the latter, lying on a gold shield, received the imposing baptism of arms.

The interlaced palms that extended over his cradle were sword-blades. His frail hand, after having touched the scepter, was attached to the hilt of a sword. Thus was presented to the people and to the army the future leader of the realm of Evir. He was named Rhamses.

But it was in a nest of rose-petals that Aurore was presented to the baptism of the mages; the softest flower petals were heaped up like down in a basket of silver filigree studded with fine pearls and the little princess, like a satin doll with enamel eyes, was curled up there, as naked as a little bird newly emerged from the egg.

She was then carried processionally through the galleries of the palace, all the way to the immense hall with large bays open to the golden backcloth of the sky, where the queen was sitting stiffly on her cathedra, in her brocade mantle, with a crown of her head, pale between her long blonde tresses, which hung to either side of her archaic visage of a virgin in a missal.

Her dreaming eyes, so soft and blue, had scanned timidly the sparkling crowd accumulated around her throne. For an instant they had reposed—oh, very indifferently—on the haughty princess whom the king loved and who resisted him, and who, cheerful, proud and also coquettish, enjoyed the martyrdom of her royal slave. Softer and sadder, however and how tenderly veiled, those divine eyes had paused on the languid face of the handsome page who loved her so much. Oh, the great dolor that passed through the soul of the little queen, immobile and fixed in her pompous pose, thinking that it would always be necessary for him to live thus, tortured, guarding a hopeless amour in his heart.

In order to collect herself she lowered her eyes, slightly moist, toward the cradle of roses where the naked little doll lay, her eyes now closed, and her heart, invaded by maternal love, was numbed somewhat in that contemplation.

The king, whose elbow was leaning non-chalantly on the royal throne, leaned back, in order that his liberated gaze could devour, without being distracted, the radiant beauty of his beloved princess, so cruel in her amused refusal.

Then the theorbs vibrated, the incense burned by the mages clouded the constellated vaults, and a great silence fell.

Through the odorous smoke, the blue tint of which embellished the bright faces of richly-adorned women similar to immortal houris, the unique circular movement of their raised arms was visible, as if they were trying to draw into the orb of their magic circles, by means of their attractive force, the scattered falling fluids of sidereal forces, and thus impart to them, by means of a rapid cohesion, a tangible form.

Soon, in fact, furrows ran through the opaque smoke, like serpentine lightning-flashes in the cloud. Vague forms emerged, immediately deformed and then renascent.

The spiral of vapors rising from the fiery tripods mutated, toward the vault, into the appearance of light bodies that rolled and blurred hectically, as if in a panic of impotent flight. There was a rip in a rapid blue light, from which a whiteness suddenly fell, like a wounded bird, which floated, with a vague sound of wings. Quickly, unfurled like the display of a vast diorama, there was a dazzling mixture of palpitating colors, fulgurant in a magical mutation, which fixed the eye in a blank stare.

Then, in the center of an enormous bloom, the multicolored flames of which spun in an endless whirl, a group of divine forms—the fays—flowered like the nascent petals of that immense rose, their floating tresses overflowing around them in a cascade of golden light.

Leaning back, hand in hand, as if for a round-dance of bacchantes, they circled ever more slowly and more visibly, even allowing to show, amid the iridescent vapor that veiled them, the dazzling whiteness of their projected breasts.

Finally, in the silence of the theorbs, the vibrations of which died away, a voice was heard, faint and musical, like that of a distant nightingale. It was a fay speaking.

"Darling," she said, pointing her finger like a pink dart toward the child sleeping in her bed of flowers, "You shall be beautiful; so beautiful that no one in the world will be able to see you without dying of amour."

"Good," murmured the king. "I know now who Aurore is going to resemble."

A second fay stretched herself, seductively, and whispered in a languid sigh: "You shall be good, kind, tender and sensitive, so compassionate that, in order not to see anyone suffering, you will grant to anyone all the gifts requested of you."

"Good," sighed the queen, who sensed the imploring gaze of the handsome page passing over her closed eyes.

A third spoke, if one can describe thus something which more closely resembled the song of breezes passing over reeds. This one promised knowledge. Another accorded the magical gift of the arts, and another that of grace and charm. Another granted her the cleverness, strength and audacity that makes heroines. And each of them, in passing, extended her open hand, and radiance flowed from her slender fingers.

Slowly, the multicolored rose shed its petals, the flames of which stirred in an endless unfurling. The divine and nacreous forms, and the flamboyant tresses of the fays kneading from golden light, gradually reentered and melted into the blue spirals of the incense smoke.

Only one luminous dot was darting a crackling tongue of vacillating fire at the fuming center of the semi-extinct rose when a sudden explosion ripped apart its blazing corolla, from which a woman emerged more beautiful, whiter and purer than the snowy marble of a Hebe. This one bore in her hand, like the stem of a lily, a wand decorated with pearls and opals, the sharp scintillating tip of which was carved into facets like a crystal fish-bone.

The new fay leaned over Aurore's cradle and said, pityingly: "I've arrived just in time for your happiness, child so poorly endowed!"

"What?" cried the king.

"What are you going to do?" moaned the gentle queen.

"Does she not have all gifts?" murmured the crowd, enumerating them: beauty, grace, mildness, goodness, charm, talents, knowledge, and even heroism! What was she lacking, then?

"She lacks," replied the fay, "the precious faculty of being able to enjoy all those gifts without each of them becoming the source of the worst dolors for her.

"What! She will be beautiful, knowledge-able and as charming as grace itself—which is to say that she will attract to herself the passionate heart whose prostration would strew the earth before here little victorious feet; and, the supreme misery, she will, at the same time, be so sensitive and compassionate that it will be necessary for her to weep—oh yes, weep, Madame la Reine—as much for the dolors to which she will give birth by her refusals as for the weaknesses of her own languid soul, as soft and tender to amour as an open flower is to the kisses of the east wind!

"What a martyrdom that life would be, for such a poorly defended heart! Everything, external or personal, would be a subject of pain for it. All the scattered evil of the world would wound it eternally. It would suffer for the most infimal suffering of beings; it would writhe in anguish for human terrors and would swoon merely in knowing about the immolation of animals, ready to die of horror at the cries of those victims of torture . . .

"Then too, nothing around her would be able to charm her. She would pass, slowly and sadly, dragging those fatal gifts, a hundred times accursed, not daring to raise to the heavens her beautiful mortal gaze, enveloping the divine grace of her body, hiding it like the excessively close splendor of a solar hearth, and hesitating even to place her foot on the ground, where innumerable living things swarm, fearing, with a tender emotion, perhaps wounding an invisible being.

"What good would it do her to have received from my imprudent sisters so many marvelous attractions, and to be thrown by them into the hectic intoxication of their waltz, if I had not come: the absolute principle of moral strength?

"And in doing this I am obeying, not pity, which is unknown to me, but the magic formula of the most savant of your mages. So here I am."

Standing tall, barely touching with the tip of her naked foot the burning heart of the rose, fuming like a cup of incense, the fay inclined her white body slowly in a nacreous curve and slowly extended toward the sleeping Aurore the scintillating tip of her wand, with the facets sculpted like a crystal fishbone, florid with pearls and opals. Then, with a swift gesture, she touched her heart.

Then, straightening up again, she started to rise in the blue spirals of the aromatic smoke clouding the vault. At the same time she dissolved, melting into a pink mist in which a tangle of gold floated.

Still scarcely visible, she murmured these words, which fell:

"Aurore, you shall be happy, for you shall be insensible. Your heart, as hard as rock crystal, will never know either pity or love . . ."

"What!" cried the king. "She will never love, nor be compassionate to those who die of love for her?"

"Never," replied the fay, vanishing with the last floating mist.

"Too bad," pronounced the king sadly, contemplating passionately his beautiful and haughty princess.

But, paling again, in the depths of her cathedra, outlined against the golden backcloth of the sky, the virginal blonde queen who was suffering so much, without looking at her page, murmured:

"So much the better!"

THE RED BIRD

BEHIND the high and somber grille the acacias were snowing. The glimpsed pathways, the bushes and the lawns faded away under the pale, soft, embalmed carpet that was raining down slowly in the breeze.

And amid that whiteness, silent shadows sometimes wandered. They passed by, brushing one another, as if without seeing one another, without interrupting the pensive fixity of their gaze or the demented strangeness of their gestures.

Some, unkempt and crowned with flowers, were dragging widespread robes with a regal air; others, their arms raised in tragic evocation, were walking with a rhythmic cadence, at a theatrical pace, retaining the pose of priestesses evoking *Yeus*. Others, weeping, their faces desolate and their arms twisted, were repeating untiringly the same terrifying sob and passing on; others, their lips red and their eyes ardent, seemed to be on the lookout, through the rose bushes, for the advent of some dear individual always expected; and they wandered, shivering with the ever-unsatisfied immortal desire that held them breathless, their hands on their hips, their mouths moist and their eyes vague. They were the patients of Dr. X*** in his sanitarium in Auteuil.

The rare visitors who had once traversed that discreet and mysterious meadow, reserved for sumptuous madwomen, will have seen one coming toward them, in the distance of the pathways, always flowery, either with the gold of ebonies in girandoles, the crimson of chestnut trees or the auroral tangle of white and red roses, disposed as on an antique statue. Her blonde and heavy hair coifs her with radiance. She walks so delicately, with a heavy and seemingly careful step, avoiding collisions, and seems to be protecting with widespread arms something invisible that she lifts up with a gesture of her advanced bosom, her torso drawn back and her back hollow. She stops close to you, puts a finger on her pale lips, and murmurs "Shh! Don't wake it!"

And if your silence reassures her, she says to you, lifting with her cupped hands the two perfect globes of her breasts of a scarcely-veiled statue: "God, how heavy it is to carry this all one's life!"

What the beautiful young blonde woman coiffed with radiance is carrying, she says, is a cage—her bosom—in which a red bird palpitates: her heart.

It is for that folly that wise men have locked her up. She consents to it, in any case, in order to be sheltered from noise and impacts that might wake the bird. She has suffered so much from her late nights. It is her who says so, speaking in a whisper.

As far back as she can remember, when she was very small, the bird sang; it jumped about in its little cadge; even its wing-beats, already rapid, made her feel ill. A cruel mother sometimes struck her, and that frightened the tender bird, which agitated hectically, as if it wanted to flee.

Later, one day, an unforgettable radiant day, the red bird sang. It sang like the chaffinches on April mornings, like the warblers on the first green sunlit branch on which flowers are budding. It sang while extending its wings and moving them gently, like oars on a blue lake; it no longer fluttered; it wept and preened itself delightedly; that was because it was no longer alone behind its veil of palpitating flesh and swollen in its fine nest of streaming crimson; another heart had come to huddle next to it. A beautiful bird, that one, valiant and terrible, but so gentle; it had given itself and wanted to remain there forever. Clinging together so closely, paralyzed in the same ecstasy, it seemed that the same slumber would cradle them for an eternity!

Speaking thus, the madwoman became resplendent; her vague gaze was illuminated broadly, arrested in a smiling and languid fixity; her mouth widened avidly and blissfully, and her hands, the fingers of which were moving slowly, paraded a nervous caress over her swelling bosom, where the invisible red bird was palpitating in its cage of quivering flesh.

Then, suddenly, her clenched fingers clutched her throat, the panting of which became increasingly rapid; her distressed face paled, and the blue-tinted circles in which her terrified eyes were wandering enlarged, devouring her cheeks. And the madwoman moaned: "Ah! Now it's flying away! It's fleeing! It's escaping me . . . ! Stop! Oh, come back, come back! What so you expect it to become without you, the one that is beating now to stifle me . . . ? Alone, alone, it will remain alone in its deserted bed! No more songs and no more amour! No more double murmurs in the voluptuous warmth of my breast, now lacerated! No more of those pecks there, so tender, which my hands feel alternating like a rhythm! No more of those dying ecstasies that suspended my breath and stopped me living in the sudden rigidity of all my bewildered being . . . oh, that gaping wound through which it fled, breaking the closed cage . . . ! Oh, that where the abandoned lies, writhing, which wounds me by striking with its reckless beak: a wound through which it, too, would like to escape! I'm in pain . . . I'm in pain . . . !"

Afterwards, she calmed down, and, resuming her pose and her careful gesture, her arms rounded in front of her breasts, now uncovered in her anguished struggle, she half-closed her weary eyelids and continued, smiling vaguely:

"Shh! It's asleep now. One day, when the intolerable pain made me writhe and howl, when I tried to break that accursed cage against a wall in order to free myself of the thing inside it that was martyrizing me, the other, which loved me so much and which has fled, came back. Yes, it came back, the inconstant, having fluttered from here to there, and regretting its nest. It came closer and, in order to get in, kissed the surroundings of its cage, here . . ."

And as, with a light finger, the madwoman brushed the florid tip of her breast, so gracious in its pose, its touching nudity and its semi-veiled whiteness, which was not the sunlight of the floating and flying gold of her hair, one might have mistaken her for a divine marble planted under the somber shadow of the flowering acacias, the odorous snow of which was raining down.

But her face, over which glided, like a cloud over a star the terrible veil of her memories, lost its smiling grace and became anxious, with a hint of mystery. And, her head tilted over the pale ivory of her bare shoulder, she seemed to be listening. To the sound of a silence she said, in a low, almost murmurous voice: "Its asleep! It always sleeps since that rhapsodic moment. Doubtless it was at the end of its strength, too weary of its long suffering, and at the very moment when happiness returned, it lost its footing in the gulf of the dream . . . it's asleep!

"You can see," she added, moving very close, offering her bare breasts, "that nothing is beating, nothing palpitating, never, never again. And I can finally rest . . . liberated! But it's necessary that it doesn't wake up . . . oh, no! Be careful. Speak in whispers, very quietly! Imagine, if it were going to wake up! I've suffered so much! That's because I remember. And I stay away, day and night, from everything noisy, everything that sings . . .

"The other day, someone passing close to these walls was playing a tune on a viol . . . oh, a tune that almost reminded me . . . and which began to stir an echo there . . . I ran away, carrying it, wrapping it in my tunic . . . So, in the evening, at sunset, I can't come this way; would you believe that there's a nightingale that calls? And so tenderly . . . oh, how scared I am . . . It's necessary that it sleeps, the red bird, forever . . . forever . . . !"

And, her arms rounded over her uplifted breast, her upper body leaning backwards, her back hollowed out by the imaginary weight of her cruel burden, the blonde madwoman coiffed with the sun's rays passed by. She went on, and disappeared into the mysterious pathways where silent phantoms were wandering. Only, from time to time, she was seen to lean over toward her unveiled heart and murmur, quietly:

"It's asleep!"

SALOME

THE coffin had been set on fire on the metal plate, and now the body was burning. It was exhaled in ardent, palpitating flames, which seemed to be alive, like the flamboyant soul of dead wood crackling in the hearth. Around the crematorium furnace the funeral aides were mopping their streaming foreheads. They only lacked the décor, the hairy nudity and the horned heads and cloven feet to resemble the demonic henchmen who stimulate the fires of Hell with their satanic tridents under the groups of the damned in Michelangelo's fresco.

Nevertheless, as if an infernal cauldron, the convulsed body appeared to be fleeing with atrocious gestures of terror the luminous torture of the sharp and caressant tongues of fire, gradually crumbling and sinking in a supreme faint. Nearby, an alabaster urn awaited the ashes.

The body thus consecrated to the flames—perhaps merited—was that of the admirable studio model who had been nicknamed Salome. Marcus the painter of pale plump blondes, seduced by that adorable antithesis, had picked her up in a market in Istanbul and brought her back with his Oriental trinkets, fabrics of golden silk, sandalwood, Damascene weapons and bottles of essences of karjanlik marked with a Byzantine cross. And for a year he had painted her, and her alone, nothing but her, always, in all poses, under all reflections. In all the corners of the studio, here under a crimson awning, there among palm-trees whose sometimes shifting shadows starred her flesh bizarrely, everywhere resplendent, her strange body stood, a finely gilded idol, sometimes veiled, with a refined science, by long silks spread over her hair, which were reminiscent of the disquieting caress of the wings of a great black swan.

Sometimes she appeared recumbent on the intense green of an improbable meadow, and the elongated form of her slender body then resembled some broken flower with a long golden calyx and somber foliage, on which two large drops of dew remained, tremulously: her eyes; and her red mouth evoked the tumultuous assemblage of a group of amorous ladybirds.

At first, Marcus, believing that he only felt an artistic passion for Salome, had consented to let her pose occasionally for the pupils of this studio. One of his friends, a young master, had also painted her, seated, hieratical and coiffed in the tiara of the Empresses of Byzantium. But suddenly, he had fallen madly in love with her; and from then on, he had hidden her from all eyes. She lived with him, buried thus in the depths of a sanctuary, intoxicated by the perfumes that he burned around her, clad like a Javanese dancer or an Annamese queen, girdled with gems, bizarrely crowned with long peacock feathers or helmeted in gold, or undressed and rubbed with saffron, her cheeks tinted with vermilion, her forehead starry, bound in a mystical bandlet. And he adored her, he possessed her, and he went mad in that incessant violation of an idol.

One clear spring night, Marcus had laid her down, naked, in a moonbeam, on the terrace of their little house in Auteuil. He had curved her like an arch, her feet joined, her arms raised above her head and bent back toward the yellow tip of her big toe; her beautiful supple flanks, taut and rounded, shining like the golden star that seemed to reflect her in the sky. And it appeared to him that the night had become brighter in the radiance of that crescent of blonde flesh.

But Salome died of it . . .

And now she was boiling in a crucible like a molten ingot. Marcus would have liked to keep her in the sarcophagus of a Ramses, a narrow body eternalized by aromatics, beautiful forever, with her painted face; to deliver that divine body to the earth seemed to him to be a profanation. Besides which, the thought of being separated from her forever gnawed his skull, and in that strange madness strange projects occurred to him. So, he decided upon incineration. Marcus possessed means of persuasion that conferred omnipotence upon him. With the aid and connivance of employees of the funereal combustion agency, he arranged a fraud: the alabaster urn would receive the ashes of the cedar-wood, and he, Marcus, would furtively take away the hot dust of Salome enclosed in a sachet of antique Indian silk.

On returning home, he deposited it on a bed strewn with rose petals and plumed with white lilac, in which the mark of the vanished body remained imprinted, long and gently hollowed out; then, with all the doors closed, he lay down in the perfumed furrow, his head buried in the warm silk sachet scented with incense and amber.

After a few nights of delirious ecstasy, however, the flowers had withered, the ashes had cooled and the perfumes had evaporated and all the subtle fragrances had vanished. Marcus, now possessed by the obsession of resurrecting Salome for himself, by means of hallucination of dream, but evoked in her color, her form and her emanations, the false intoxications of which had been lacking in order to live, as if he had lost the breath. Marcus sensed a demented discovery germinating in the fissures of his brain, crushed between his fists.

During his grim comings and goings overlooking the gardens undergoing the labor of renewal, a work had struck him, soon fixed in his mind in the initial form of the gesture. Halted, his finger to his forehead and his gaze fixed, he had allowed it to inscribe within himself the image replacing the idea.

One morning, like a laborer who gets up at dawn in order to go and sow his fields, Marcus went down, with a spade over his shoulder, to the as-yet-uncultivated area in his garden. With a rhythmic, almost unconscious movement, he opened the earth, striping it with bizarre furrows that resembled cross-hatching traced with charcoal for a sketch. Then he took handfuls of light seed from an antique sachet of Indian silk and cast it in front of him over the gaping furrows, with a fine flourish of his arm, extended in the superb thrust of a sower.

Marcus spent his days thereafter crouching next to the earth that he had inseminated with Salome's ashes, and he waited gravely.

For a long time, that plot, among others that were verdant and florid, remained black; the other uncultivated plots had sprouted vegetation freely, at the hazard of seeds brought by the wind, fallen from the beaks of sparrows or scattered by the wings of bees. That one, covered as if by a shroud, seemed dead.

Summer came. Then, one day, as he approached, Marcus uttered a hoarse cry and fell to his knees. Then, with his face lowered to the ground and his eyes dilated, he sniffed a scarcely visible and scarcely green efflorescence of three shoots which had finally sprouted from the soil; he kissed them and watered them with sudden tears, streaming like a rainstorm. Reassured, Marcus became calm again; he had understood: that daughter of the sun could only be reborn by means of the hot fecundation of the sunlight. Now she was about to grow, to blossom, to embalm him and give him once again all the voluptuous joys the privation of which was killing him.

And as everything grew around him, the wheat raising its stems, the gladioli and the lilies springing from the soil. Thus, Marcus thought, Salome was going to rise, a regal and triumphant flower, which would soon elevate the incomparable glory of its golden calyx toward the incomparable heavens.

The tranquil dementia of Marcus had permitted him to be left undisturbed in his house in Auteuil. He was reckoned to love and to be cultivating his flowers, and it was judged that that occupation was good for him.

He was therefore able, as he wished to spend all his hours next to the mound on which a vegetation of little leaves was developing, short, hard and bushy, devoid of stems. Then that growth ceased, and the little tufts formed tight buds. Then the buds opened, almost all together, in a single night. And in the morning, Marcus, who came running, tottered, faint with joy; Salome was there. She was there, as on the day when he had laid her down in a ray of moonlight, her curving body closing a golden crescent. Just as he had designed her with furrows dug with his spade, so she had bloomed. It was her, and Marcus had finally found her again.

He knelt down, his mouth agape with gasping laughter, and he began speaking to her in a low voice. How well he reognized in that florid body all the beauties of his beloved, even the most secret! How veritably all those little blonde pansies,[1] delicately shaded, were formed from the velvety flesh of Salome; they were clad in gleaming silk. Here and there, darker in color and bushier, they emphasized the shadows more brightly bursting forth like the protrusion of breasts, raised hips and luminous knees. They too, lying in their somber foliage, seemed to be enveloped by the blue waves of their immense hair, as caressant as the urgent wings of a great black swan.

And their intimate womanly perfume was exhaled, intoxicating, and finished plunging Marcus' mind into a profound darkness devoid henceforth of dawns. Leaning over on his hands, his nostrils snuffling, he started crawling toward his extended prey. He sniffed her, swooning, as if at the scents of a body; he stretched his neck and brushed with his open mouth all those little saffroned flow-

---

1 The French *pensées* [pansies], also means "thoughts"; an alternative name for the flower in question, in English, is heartsease.

ers, blonde pupils of an embalmed flesh that seemed tremulous.

He crawled, rising to the face. And the Salome of flowers seemed to watch him coming; two large black pansies striped her bright inverted face, while a strange red palpitating patch was reminiscent of a mouth murmuring an amorous appeal.

Then Marcus, suddenly bewildered by desire, extended his arms and hurled himself, bestially, upon the entire floraison of pansies, crushing them and violating them. And crying: "Salome!" he fell upon the dying red lips. But at the slight sound of ladybirds' wings, which brushed his mouth as they flew off, Marcus believing that he felt the breath of a kiss mingle with his own breath, fainted in a supreme spasm and expired, delirious with joy.

A PARTIAL LIST OF SNUGGLY BOOKS

Lightning Source UK Ltd.
Milton Keynes UK
UKHW010642110521
383528UK00001B/203

9 781645 250616